I0451111

MONSTER UNDER YOUR BED

Amy Hoff

Caledonia #5

Erebus Society

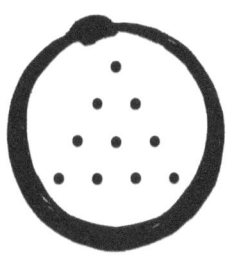

Erebus Society

First published in Great Britain in 2023
Erebus Society

First Edition

ISBN: 978-1-912461-53-0

www.ErebusSociety.com

TABLE OF CONTENTS

LOST WEEKEND

MONSTER UNDER YOUR BED

CHAPTER ONE

The Apartments

Paris was beautiful in the spring, but then, Paris was beautiful at any time of the year.

It had been an age since Dorian Grey had graced the boulevards of that grand city. He was mildly surprised to find himself here at all.

When Robert Burns had asked if he'd like to join their fortunes and move in together, this was not what he had expected. But Robert had insisted the best thing they could do with their respective situations was to go elsewhere for a while.

Dorian conceded he certainly needed a holiday. He hadn't expected to find himself in the same rooms he had once occupied in Paris over a century ago. That was a brilliant and beautiful Paris, a Paris of everyone's dreams, but a Paris long ago consigned to history.

Strange, how the most scintillating times of history seem to happen just before a major calamity. World War I removed much of the beauty from the world, just as World War II would later remove much of its social progress and acceptance of men like Dorian Grey.

But Paris, dear Paris, was indefatigable, was beautiful in the long-suffering but resilient arrogance of itself, and Dorian had always loved the place. Not for the romanticism most placed upon it; he had read that there were free helplines for tourists to call and complain about just how *awful* Paris was, but it was the awfulness in and of itself that appealed to the selkie. Something about a beautiful façade and a questionable interior spoke to Dorian's soul in a way most cities never did.

Dorian Grey was of Seal-Hame, of the Scottish Highlands, and like many Highlanders, he had found himself beneath the Hielanman's Umbrella of Glasgow Central Station, but at heart he had never felt Glaswegian.

Dorian Grey was a selkie in search of a home.

***

The rooms of his old apartments were just as he'd remembered.

They'd even left all the original paintings.

"It's historical," the realtor told him, to justify the extreme price.

Dorian didn't care.

This was the place he used to visit all those years ago.

Before Dahlia, before Aidan, before what he'd done to Desdemona.

Just...*before.*

And Robert was there, just as he had been in London, all those years ago.

The study was filled to the brim with antique furniture. It was accessed through two glass French doors. There was a balcony overlooking the city, but nothing else overlooked the balcony.

Dorian allowed himself a half-smile at the memories he had made on the balcony, before the world had gotten so loud and busy.

There were bedrooms off the hallway and a tiny kitchen as well. Paris had never been much on palatial spaces, at least outside of the palace itself.

But for Dorian, it had been enough.

A cool breeze moved the curtains. It was so strange, how much had changed and yet how much remained the same. Rome was the Eternal City, but Dorian felt Paris was immortal.

And he would know.

Dorian stood at the window, looking outside. The new buds were on the trees, just turning, and the wrought-iron balconies across the way bloomed with various plants and flowers.

He sighed, his mind on too many things at once.

"Something wrong?"

He half-turned to see Robert closing the front door, his arms filled with bread and pastries from the corner bakery. The scent was always tantalising; Dorian had been a customer for over one hundred years. He often wondered if any of the people working in that particular *pâtisserie* had noticed the slight, handsome young man in the Victorian waistcoats, with his huge dark eyes and his slick black hair, never seemed to age.

Perhaps they had noticed, but being Parisian, which was like being French but doubly so, deigned to avoid comment.

Dorian smiled at Robert, although his smile was tinged with sadness. He inspected the box of pastries, with their beautiful artistic flair, and was impressed once again with human ingenuity that even extended to their dessert foods, something the Fae couldn't even begin to fathom.

Like us, thought Dorian, *these are the result of human imagination.*

He selected a *religieuse*, a type of puff pastry reminiscent of a nun, with elaborate chocolate designs. He thought it a pity to eat such artwork.

But then, that is its purpose, he thought, as he ate it anyway.

"What is it, Dorian?" asked Robert, who seemed less interested in the artistic merit of the pastries and was just eating them without much consideration. "You can talk to me, I'll listen."

"Nothing new," Dorian replied. "In for the day?"

"If I don't want to be immolated," said Robert, throwing himself into an overstuffed armchair with the kind of insouciant beauty Oscar Wilde had once ascribed to Dorian, in his strange little tale about a man whose true inner beauty was displayed in the ugly portrait hidden in an attic, decaying against the wall.

Oscar was more perceptive than he had known.

"Why are you eating that?" asked Dorian. "I can't imagine it tastes like much to you."

Robert shrugged as he ate.

"I once loved chocolate," he said. "I miss it. You're right; it doesn't really taste of anything much, but I can't imagine it'll hurt. Go ahead."

He pushed the bag toward Dorian, who reluctantly took it.

"You've always been supernatural," said Robert. "Maybe you wouldn't understand, but there are things about mortal life I miss."

"Would you have preferred to remain mortal?" asked Dorian, pulling an éclair out of the bag. "The thing about French pastry is that you must appreciate it as art as well as food. I imagine as a vampire you might enjoy the visual feast more than the literal one."

Robert looked at him, and Dorian was once again arrested by the strange colour of his eyes. Even before Robert had become a vampire, the colour and intensity of his gaze had been unsettling indeed.

Like whisky on fire, Leah had said, during one of her wilder nights down at Waxy's –

Dorian gave his head a violent shake. He wouldn't think of her.

He couldn't. His mental state was on shaky ground as it was.

"Funny," said Robert, chewing slowly. "I wrote a lot about heartbreak. The romantic kind. But never about the pain of losing a best friend."

Dorian swallowed, wondering if his thoughts were so obvious.

"You're not obvious to most," Robert said, as if Dorian had spoken, "but I've been told I'm particularly perceptive when it comes to love."

"Indeed," said Dorian mildly, and turned toward the window again.

***

The days were long and quiet, the two men performing an unspoken ballet around each other. They shared the same space, but as if each of them treated the other as a ghost.

Dorian felt Robert was being too careful with him, as if he

were breakable.

"Robert," he said, stopping him as he haunted the corridors.

Standing in the shadows of the sunlight pouring into the house, he was a study in black and white.

"Dorian?" said Robert, a gentle lift of the word, like a question mark.

"I have made mistakes in my life," said Dorian. "They were so long ago."

Robert stared at him.

"Not so long ago as that," he said, his voice edged with anger. "Your actions alone caused suffering to all of us, me included. You wanted to do the right thing, and in doing so, damned us all."

Dorian's head bowed with the weight of the world, and all the things he had done, on his shoulders. He turned to look through the glass doors at the city in motion beyond the balcony while Robert stayed in the deep shadows.

"Oscar always said Paris was beautiful this time of year," Dorian murmured. "I miss him."

Robert nodded.

"As do I," he said.

Dorian lifted his head and looked at his friend.

"And I miss Leah," he said, loud and clear.

He hadn't said her name aloud in months.

They had avoided the topic; Robert keeping a respectful distance from it, Dorian wanting to ignore it, as if that would make it all go away.

Dorian pulled the heavy curtains closed and walked into the salon. Robert followed.

"Iain once told me something," said Robert. "About Des. About love."

"I thought Iain couldn't love," said Dorian.

"That's just the thing," said Robert. "He could, after a fashion. And he told me he loved Desdemona as much as I did, maybe more. Platonic love is just as intense, for some."

"Selkies are made for love," mused Dorian. "Maybe it's not

only romantic."

Robert nodded.

"And you love your brother," he said.

Dorian's mouth was a hard line.

"Magnus is a serial killer."

"What am I, then?" asked Robert. "I'm a vampire, Dorian. You know what vampires have to do to survive."

"There's a difference between nature and murdering people because you *can*," said Dorian.

"Sure," said Robert. "But we're all monsters, like Milo always says. I don't know, Dorian. Can you be forgiven, for your inaction? For the things you didn't do, that led to the things Magnus has done?"

"Even if I could be, I don't think I can forgive myself," said Dorian, between his teeth.

He was startled by a gentle touch. Robert tipped his chin up with his fingers.

"I forgive you," Robert said, and kissed him.

CHAPTER TWO

Touchstone

What are you doing?!"

Dorian reared back and his legs hit the couch as he sat down hard.

But Robert was still advancing, a strangely predatory gleam in his eye.

Dorian wondered if this was what his victims saw just before.

He put his hand out.

"Robert," he said. "What –"

Robert, mercifully, stopped. He sighed.

"When we were on Oscar's ship," he began, staring at a space above Dorian's head. "I don't know, Dorian. It's not like it would be the first time."

Now Dorian was really confused.

"What do you mean?"

Robert frowned.

"You don't remember," he said flatly. "Our *lost weekend*. In London?"

"I –"

Something in Dorian's mind was jarred loose.

"There was a memory," he said slowly. "When I was at MI-18. You – and I. We – but then it was Aidan. It was all very confusing."

Robert cupped Dorian's face in his hand.

"Drugs," he said, as if it explained everything. Maybe it did. "Neither of us will ever love the way we could have. But we can have this, I think."

"I wish I could remember," said Dorian, now looking up into Robert's eyes, mesmerised by the amber colour there, as the light played in their facets.

"Will you?" husked Robert, drawing a thumb down the line

of Dorian's jaw. "We could find comfort in one another. If you want."

Wordlessly, Dorian nodded his assent.

And Robert kissed him again.

***

Dorian's bare skin glowed in the late morning light, thrown into contrast and illuminated by the windows.

"Richard taught me, as he called them, *the secrets of love*," Robert whispered. "Oh, he denied it later, mostly because it made him sound like a womanizer. But no one knew what he truly meant. He taught me everything I know."

Dorian sat up, pooled in the rumpled white sheets of the bed.

"I wish there was more I could offer you," he said. "Once Taken, a selkie's heart can belong to no other."

"Hmm," said Robert, into the skin at the juncture of Dorian's neck and shoulder. "Yes, I know the story. But stories can change."

"We aren't the ones capable of changing," said Dorian, lost in a sigh.

"Sebastian changed his story," said Robert. "Maybe we can, too."

Dorian pulled away from him and shot him a hard look.

"Then you would forget Desdemona?" he asked.

The light in Robert's strange preternatural eyes dimmed.

"Never," he said. "But I had other women, other loves. None like I feel for Des, of course, but I found solace in others, and they in me."

"I doubt I can," said Dorian. "Aidan, Dahlia, they were – they were *mine*, Robert. Now, what do I have?"

"You have Leah," said Robert. Dorian scoffed. "Give her time. She'll return to you. She'll forgive."

Robert smiled.

"I did."

"You're a vampire," said Dorian. "It's different."

"She's a drunk," said Robert. "We all have our crosses to bear."

He pulled Dorian to himself and kissed him, over his eyelids, his dark hair.

"You are beautiful," he murmured. "One of the most beautiful creatures I have ever seen."

He kissed down Dorian's chest, making him pant.

"And I forgive you. I forgive you. I forgive you."

Dorian fell back into the softness of the bed and understood exactly why Robert had been so popular with the women.

And apparently the men, although this was news to him.

Not for the first time in his long existence, Dorian Grey wished he had opium.

But he wanted to remember, this time.

***

"*It ne'er was wealth, it ne'er was wealth,*
That coft contentment, peace, or pleasure;
The bands and bliss o' mutual love,
O that's the chiefest warld's treasure," Dorian quoted.

Robert rolled over and smiled.

"Where'd you hear that?"

Dorian closed his eyes, embarrassed.

"I might have read some of your work," he admitted.

He opened one eye to see Robert grinning at him.

"Don't start," Dorian warned, when Robert pulled him closer.

"I *knew* it," said Robert, nuzzling into his neck.

"I wouldn't get any ideas," Dorian warned.

"You're not my usual food, Dorian," said Robert. He popped up with the same proud grin. "I knew you read my poetry."

"Kind of hard to miss," grumbled Dorian, blushing.

"I'm flattered," said Robert.

"I should have kept my mouth shut," said Dorian, but he was smiling, and the room was filled with life and light, for the first time in a while.

The world had seemed lifeless, colourless, like an airless

room, for so long.

Now things were different. His soul felt lighter than before.

He caught Robert's gaze and they both stilled, staring at each other.

He suddenly recognised the feeling. It had been so many years that it had taken him some time to realise what it meant.

"Is this –"

"Do you –"

Stunned, they both nodded slowly.

They both feared to speak, to chase away this strange new fragile thing.

"Do you think it's because of Sebastian?" said Robert, barely breathing. "Because he broke out of his story?"

Dorian shook his head. Of this, he was absolutely certain.

"No," he said. "It's because of Leah."

CHAPTER THREE

Human Remains

Yeah? Are you sure?"

Dorian nodded, confidence flooding through him as the world gained colour again, feeling the ancient magic deep inside his soul.

A selkie's purpose is love.

It is also his power.

"Leah's changed everything before," said Dorian. "She's not limited by story."

"So you think her proximity to us...changed things?" asked Robert.

Dorian shrugged.

"Or she's done something," he said. "Throw a human into the mix, you never know what will happen. God knows what she's been up to in Glasgow while we've been away."

Robert reached out to touch him, then dropped his hand.

"I didn't mean –" he said. "I can see your value, Dorian, I don't need a spell to do it."

"But would you?" asked Dorian, scarcely daring to believe.

"Would I?" parroted Robert, although it was clear he knew what the question would be.

"Would you want a life where things changed?" asked Dorian, hesitant. "Where you could feel again. Something new."

Robert's breath came out jagged. Fear clouded his eyes.

"I don't know," he admitted. "I've always just been – this. In love with Desdemona. It's who I am. Who I've always been."

"Doesn't need to be," said Dorian. "Maybe even old dogs can learn."

"Maybe," said Robert, but it came out on a sigh.

This time, when they kissed, there was not just comfort in it, but passion.

***

A low buzz sounded, somewhere in the room.

"What's that?" mumbled Robert, muzzy with love.

"I don't – oh," said Dorian, distracted. "My phone. Text message."

"Leave it," said Robert. "It'll be there later."

"I can't, you know that," Dorian admonished, wrapping himself in the bedding as he hopped out to check. "It's from Leah."

"Oh?"

Robert stretched out on the bed, luxuriating in the late afternoon breeze coming from the windows, languorous and proud.

"She says there's something happening in Glasgow," Dorian read out.

"When isn't there?"

"Something to do with Aoife's daughter," explained Dorian.

"Does Leah need us?" asked Robert.

"She says she'll let us know," said Dorian.

He frowned.

"What's wrong?"

"No emojis."

Robert's eyebrow arched.

"And?"

"She usually leaves me emojis."

"Come back to bed, Dorian Grey."

***

Dorian was cradled in Robert's arms when he finally confessed.

"I was blacked out," he said. "I'd tried to quit, I really had. For Dahlia. But the moment I got a taste – it was like a fire was lit inside me, engulfing me from within. I couldn't get enough."

"Kindling, they call it nowadays," Robert told him. Dorian raised an eyebrow. "If you quit for a long time, just a taste can make you fall into madness for some reason. They say it about alcohol, and it was true for me. I assume the same could be said for other drugs. Do you know what became of Dahlia, in the end?"

"I don't remember," admitted Dorian. "Any of it. Although I saw the aftermath."

He closed his eyes briefly.

"The only hint I had was when I had those visions. And I certainly didn't remember until that point. It was only vague and hazy. Nobody is going to listen to the word of an addict."

"I lost a great deal of my own life to alcohol," Robert said. "I can't say it wasn't your fault, any more than it wasn't my own fault. But your fault was in succumbing to the temptation of the drug and blacking out. There's a difference between hiding a murderer and being enslaved to a substance."

"That's just it," said Dorian, wretched. "Desdemona was probably the worst addict of us all, and she has no such history."

"That we know of," Robert supplied. "I may be a man in love, Dorian, but I'm also not stupid. There are many possibilities when drugs of any kind are involved. It's water under the bridge now anyway. We must not focus on the men we were, but on the men we wish to be. The events of Burns Night taught me that, at least."

"You are so aggressively optimistic," said Dorian. "I don't know how you do it."

"Melancholy was always the worst part of my nature," said Robert. "I prefer to avoid it if I can. And I prefer to keep learning, as life continues, and I've been gifted so much of it. We all must be capable of change."

"Perhaps you're right," said Dorian.

"I know I am," said Robert.

"I didn't remember, you know. The *lost weekend,* as you call it."

"You mean us? Last time?"

Dorian turned in the bed.

"Yes, that," he said. "And it was muddled up with Aidan, somehow. Sometimes I think I didn't live most of my life. Just sidled along in a drug haze. Now it seems I'm waking up."

"Since Leah."

Dorian nodded.

"Since Leah."

"Friendship can create bonds as strong as love," said Robert. "Even stronger, sometimes."

"Leah would say you were a *sap*."

"And she has, many times. But I thought you gave up all those vices of yours after Dahlia?"

"I did," said Dorian. "But I never felt really *alive* before."

"For what it's worth," said Robert, "I hope you two can patch things up."

"As do I," sighed Dorian. "And what of you? And Desdemona? You do realise she's mostly made of smoke?"

"Aye," grinned Robert, flopping back onto the bed. "But you must admit, there has never been anything like her in the world before, and probably never will be again."

"She is unique. It's true."

"And this?" asked Robert, unsure, laying a hand against Dorian's bare chest. "What of it? A strange new thing, a butterfly out of its chrysalis."

"I don't know," said Dorian. "But I do know Leah would say *well don't poke at it*. Let things be."

Robert nodded, and then pulled Dorian into another kiss, as if he couldn't get enough.

And maybe he couldn't.

"Bread and water, Dorian," he gasped between kisses. "Bread and water, for three hundred years."

***

"So you think she somehow, what, crowbarred you open?" asked Robert, afterward. "It's a theory. I'll give you that."

"*Us*, Robert," said Dorian. "All of us."

"Don't look at me," said Robert airily. "I hardly fraternise with you people."

"Oh?" asked Dorian. "And what was Burns Night, then?"

"Unavoidable," said Robert.

"You enjoyed it. Admit it," said Dorian.

"Yes, I certainly enjoyed being trapped by Des and nearly being eaten."

"You enjoyed that too."

Robert sighed.

"Fine. A man can have strange tastes. There's no shame in it! I read a book."

"Did ye aye."

"Oh, all right, a website," Robert relented.

"Indeed," said Dorian drily. "And just what *kind* of website, Robert Burns? The kind you delete from your browser?"

Robert's jaw dropped.

"How did you –"

"As I have informed Miss Bishop on several occasions, I am up-to-date with modern culture," sniffed Dorian.

"Yes? And you watch creature videos on the externet?" asked Robert. "Leah told me."

"I certainly visit different websites than you do."

"Oh, come on, I know you have a waistcoat fetish –"

"Now is not the time to discuss my proclivities."

"Now is the perfect time! We're in Paris," said Robert, pulling him close again. "And what's more – we're in bed."

"Oscar would have a field day."

"Then let's have one in his honour."

CHAPTER FOUR

Paris

The city was busy, but the scent of the flowers was carried on the wind.

"Nice," said Robert. "You know, Paris is not as romantic as Oscar said. First of all, there's the smell."

"Well, we're from the Scottish countryside," said Dorian. "There's not much in the way of industry up there, after all. Cities smell. Glasgow doesn't exactly smell of roses."

Robert took Dorian's hand and smiled.

"It does in Kelvingrove Park."

"You know as well as I do the kinds of things that go on in Kelvingrove Park."

"For a selkie, you're not very romantic," said Robert.

"And for a poet, you're far too optimistic."

"Oscar was both, you know," said Robert. "He's been on my mind since we arrived. Should we pay him a visit?"

"I regret to inform you that our dear friend Oscar has since shuffled off this mortal coil."

"So have I."

"True."

They found themselves in Père Lachaise soon enough and made their way to Oscar Wilde's tomb.

"Ostentatious," said Dorian.

"As was Oscar," said Robert.

"Ridiculous. Look at all these lipstick marks. Vandals!"

"I feel that Oscar would approve."

"Ah, gentlemen!" said a voice. "I had wondered when you would grace my grave with your presence."

They turned to see a rather rotund man with boyish curls, dressed in his finery and leaning against a cane.

"It's only taken, what? A hundred years?"

The man *tch*ed at them, but he was smiling.

"*Oscar?!*" they both said. Oscar bowed deeply.

"If you've been a ghost all this time, why didn't you come and visit?" asked Dorian.

"Oh, but I did!" said Oscar. "You've been hosted by my nephew Oisín, I believe? And you saw my pleasure yacht?"

"That was real?"

"Real as things are for things like us. I wasn't about to let you boys have all the fun. Vampire, selkie – ghost! The position wasn't filled, and I do so love a bogey-tale! Besides, some handsome young men do indeed come here and kiss my headstone, so I certainly wasn't about to miss that."

He sighed, leaning on his cane.

"I *do* miss the boys," he said. "And the champagne. Undeath is, well, a bit boring."

"You could've alerted Gallia Interpol," said Dorian. "It's right here in Paris!"

Oscar shrugged.

"I was having fun appearing to handsome young men," said Oscar. "And other things. You know we're not as insubstantial as all that, of course. And there are plenty of beautiful young men who are all in on the idea of sex with the ghost of Oscar Wilde."

Dorian stared at the ground and Oscar laughed.

"Scotsmen are so hilariously British," he said. "Repressed. Irish men, not so much. Contributed to my downfall in London, I'm sure. Anyway, it was all harmless fun, what interest could Gallia have in that? French monster Interpol needs to get on over to the graveyard and stop some young twink having sex with the shade of Wilde? I think my lovers might have objected, and besides, it's so on-brand for Paris, isn't it? Besides, I was hoping to see one of you again. It would've spoiled the surprise. Though you certainly took your time about it."

Oscar *tsk*ed at them again, but there was no real feeling behind it.

Then he spied their hands, linked together. His eyes flew open.

"Be still my beating heart!" shouted Oscar. "Is it true? In all my years, I never! You simply *must* interrupt my nattering with such a momentous occasion!"

Robert smiled softly.

"We don't know, Oscar," he said. "Things have been rough of late, and we decided it would be best to –"

"Find comfort in each other, of course, of course," Oscar said, waving it away. "I would expect no less from two hedonists like yourselves. Only, it seems, things have changed? I take it this is more than comfort? You both look decidedly confused."

The two of them nodded mutely.

"I still love Desdemona with everything I am," said Robert.

"And I, both Aidan and Dahlia," Dorian supplied.

"But?"

The two of them looked at each other, then down at the ground.

"Bashful?" teased Oscar. "This is certainly new."

"That's just it, Oscar," said Robert. "It's *new*. We've known each other for centuries, and this isn't the first time we've –"

"Found comfort in each other," Dorian supplied.

"I cannot tell you how delighted I am to hear that," said Oscar. "I always knew I would make a wonderful matchmaker. I'm thrilled that I was right; what man doesn't want to be? But you're correct in your suspicions. We're stories, after all, and stories cannot change."

"But humans can change them," said Dorian. "After all, it's why Aonghas's clothing changes year to year. It's why Sebastian was able to break out of his own story – he was human first."

"As was I," said Robert. "As were you, Oscar."

Oscar leaned against his headstone, thinking.

"But Dorian wasn't," he said. "What does it mean, if he's *feeling things* too?"

"I hate to *poke at it*, as my – as Leah would say," said Dorian, unable to keep the pain from his expression. "I don't want to lose it."

"It's a very human thing, isn't it?" asked Oscar.

"What's that?"

"Hope."

The two men stared at Oscar for a while, stunned.

"Oh, come now, boys," said Oscar. "And if you'd like to demonstrate for me later, I'd be up for it. But we're from two of the saddest nations with the saddest, most hopeless stories in the world. A vampire cursed to love the same creature for the rest of time, knowing that said creature can never love him in return? And the selkies are the same, but across their entire species. Seal-Hame must be creaking at the seams with selkies whose loves are gone, for one reason or another. If this isn't limited to the two of you – hell, even if it is – this is the first glimmer of hope in centuries. Change can be a good thing."

"Does that mean Desdemona might," Robert said, his eager words nearly swallowed back in his throat.

"Who knows?" said Oscar. "It could be a permanent truth for her. But the takeaway from this is that there's a whole *possibility* of stories that can write themselves, now. And it's hope we had no business wishing for, because our stories were written in stone, so long ago."

"Do you know why this might be happening?" asked Robert.

"I think it's Leah's doing," said Dorian. "Not on purpose, of course, but we don't usually spend that amount of time around humans."

"Perhaps you're onto something there," said Oscar. "But we'll talk better at the Café de la Paix, if it's still open. Yes? Capital. Let's go."

"Go? Aren't you a ghost?" asked Robert.

Oscar turned.

"Yes, and it seems I can choose the places I haunt," he said. "Much like your resident ghost witch, Hazel, I think? Come along, boys, time's wasting."

CHAPTER FIVE

Champagne

The place looked splendid, as it always had. Dorian did not share Oscar's love of ostentation, but he had to admit there was an element of stylishness missing from the modern day.

"Would you consider coming to work for Chief Ben at Interpol, Oscar?" asked Dorian.

"Oh, you know me, boys," he said with a wink. "I was never one for *work*, how positively gauche."

"Then what will you do?"

"What I've always done," he said. "Happiness is in being satisfied with your lot, and I am always satisfied here."

"Besides," he continued, with a meaningful look at Robert, "you already have a resident poet."

"I don't work for Interpol," protested Robert.

"If you say so, old chap," said Oscar. Then he turned to address the waiter.

"Champagne, please, for myself and my friends," he said.

"Very good, sir," nodded the waiter in English, all of which was very strange.

"He doesn't seem surprised that you're a ghost," Robert pointed out.

"He doesn't seem unimpressed that you're speaking English," said Dorian. "Parisian waiters are famous for their rudeness. This one is letting the side down."

"Oh, don't be ridiculous, boys," said Oscar. "Pierre here is a ghost, too. Gives him a sense of purpose, you see."

Dorian looked around at the other patrons.

"And nobody seems to mind?"

"They're French, Dorian," said Oscar. "Even if they did mind, they wouldn't *say* anything about it. Politics, riots, bread – all these are things that concern the Frenchman. Ghosts, in a city built on catacombs? Just another Tuesday."

"I thought you hadn't been to this café in some time," Robert accused.

"And I haven't," said Oscar. "That's the thing about Paris, and ghosts. Both are eternal."

"You've always got an answer for everything," smiled Dorian. "I have missed you, Oscar."

"While I do enjoy a bit of flattery with my appetizers," said Oscar, "I think we need to discuss what is happening here, and the end result."

"End result?" asked Robert, as Pierre returned to pour the champagne and then leave the bottle in the silver ice bucket beside them. "What do you mean?"

"All things of this nature have a price," said Oscar. "For example, your little foray into mortality on Burns Night. You *chose* to return to the supernatural world. You didn't have to."

"Are you saying you think this is a curse, and we'll be forced to make a choice, in the end?" asked Dorian. "I've suspected the same."

"No, I can't say I think it's magic," he said. "I think it's the opposite of magic. I think it's the first time in a long time that real, human life has intersected with your own. And there will most likely come a time in which you must choose, Dorian Grey. Magic or the mundane?"

"I've been magic long enough," said Dorian. "I had forgotten, how intoxicating and exciting this is, the first sensation of falling."

"I did nothing but write poetry about that very thing for years," said Robert, who then started. "Does this mean – *yes! I can write poetry again!*"

He was up and out of his chair in search of a pen and some paper before either of his companions could say anything.

"It's probably going to be hideous," said Oscar. "He's out of practice, after all."

Oscar sniffed at his champagne before drinking it with evident gusto.

"Dorian," he said, "between you and me – there's far more you'd be giving up besides magic. Immortality."

"I've had a long life, Oscar," said Dorian.

"And the ability to help your partner, Leah," said Oscar. "There are things that an immortal, nearly-invulnerable being can do that a mere mortal cannot."

This sobered Dorian quite a bit.

"So in the end, you'll have to ask yourself," Oscar said, "if you're willing to sacrifice everything in order to gain the mortal world. For the option of options, shall we say."

Dorian sat back with his own glass of champagne and contemplated Oscar's words, as the people of Paris came and went from one of its oldest cafés, and Robert returned with a new sonnet composed that very moment.

Oscar was right. It was terrible.

But that didn't really matter.

The look of pride on his face, the excitement in his eyes – Dorian felt it again, that wonderful feeling of first love, but it was coloured with the strange certainty that something evil must be behind it all.

At the end of the day, Dorian Grey was a detective.

And it was becoming clearer and clearer that this simply could not be a gift from out of the blue.

It was a mystery, and mysteries needed solving.

***

"Dorian, are you serious?" Robert demanded, as they walked back to their apartments. "Can't you let go of work for *one day*?"

"I did," said Dorian. "Look where it's led us."

"What about Leah always saying *well don't poke at it*?" Robert reasoned. "And here you are, doing exactly that!"

"Robert, I would like nothing more than for this to be real," said Dorian, as he reached their door. "But we also need to be realistic. This is completely unexpected!"

He turned the key in the lock and went inside.

Robert followed him.

"You say that, but I don't believe you," he said. "I think you're scared."

"Scared?" Dorian scoffed, turning on a light. "Why would I be scared? Selkies are supposed to fall in love."

"And you thought you were finished with all that!" said Robert. "It's *safe*, hiding in your story. I think it terrifies you, the idea things might change forever, and you might get hurt!"

"I can't trust something that just fell from heaven," argued Dorian. "This is completely unprecedented!"

"And it's completely normal!" said Robert. "Believe me, I did it often enough! Falling in love. It's a human thing."

"But I'm *not human*," Dorian said. "And yes, I know you used to be. But the fact that this is affecting me as well means that something is up. You *know* it, Robert. You've seen Leah and me at work."

Sighing, Robert threw himself into the nearest chair. He leaned his head back against it, and put his arm across his eyes.

"Can't we just, I don't know, do this for a while?" he asked. Then he sat up. "Wait. How do we know it isn't Oscar causing it? I mean, he was behind it last time, on his ghost ship."

"I think Oscar would have owned up by now," said Dorian. "No, I think he was onto something, back on that pleasure-cruise. That we might have gravitated towards one another, if circumstances were different."

"But circumstances *are* different," said Robert. "What's changed?"

"One thing has changed."

"Leah."

"I don't know how, but I still feel that our friendship is at the crux of this matter," said Dorian. "Mine and Leah's. Our friendship, and the loss of it."

Robert reached out and gathered Dorian into his lap. He kissed him senseless.

"But for now," Robert whispered. "Let's have this, together."

Dorian's stiff upper lip could only last so long.

"For now," he murmured, and lost himself in Robert's kisses.

CHAPTER SIX

The Opposite of Magic

There must be someone we can ask."

Robert and Dorian were walking beside the Seine as the Eiffel Tower sparkled in the night.

"Paris is lovely this evening," said Dorian.

"What if," Robert said, hesitant. Dorian turned to look at him.

"What if it's like Oscar says?" said Robert. "No mystery. No nothing. Just, *the opposite of magic*. Real life. Normal life. Nothing changes for us, except the curse is broken."

Dorian stared at him.

"Then," he said. "Then – I don't know, Robert. It's frightening."

"Then let it be frightening," said Robert. "This is how most people live. There are no guarantees."

"It's just...I've lived like this for so long," said Dorian. "What if it's worse, the other way?"

"Well, then it's worse?" said Robert. "But there's also a chance it could be better. We've tried it one way for all these centuries. Why not try something new?"

"I find myself uncertain," muttered Dorian. "It's risky."

"It's Plato's allegory of the cave," said Robert, warming to his theme. "Do you want the shadows on the wall, or do you want to go out into the sunlight?"

"If you go out into the sunlight you'll burn to a crisp," said Dorian.

"Okay, bad analogy," said Robert. "But still, Dorian – *hope*. When was the last time we had it? And if things are worse later, we can also *make them better*. We'll have freedom, either way. What do you say? Will you jump?"

"How are you so relentlessly romantic and cheerful?" asked

Dorian. "It's unbecoming, and frankly not very Scottish of you."

Robert hit him with his trademark million-watt grin.

"Come on, you love it," he said. "And you know why? Because it's *hope*, Dorian Grey."

"You're insufferable."

"You want to wither away in an attic, that's your lookout," said Robert. "But it's been *centuries* since I had a taste of this. Love was always my favourite drug."

"And look where it got you!" said Dorian. "I'm sorry, Robert, I just can't trust it. Any of this!"

"Honestly, it seems like you *want* it to be some kind of magic!" said Robert. "A spell, a curse, anything."

"Because this *isn't* normal, for us!" insisted Dorian. "We both live inside the parameters of our stories. Any change usually means something terrible is about to happen!"

"Just once," said Robert, "I'd like it to be *good* news."

"So would I," said Dorian gently. "But I've been a detective for a long time, Robert, and my instincts tell me something's wrong here."

"Fine," said Robert. "Then let's get to the bottom of this. Any idea where we can go, who we can ask? Would Gallia Interpol be able to help?"

"No, this isn't really a police matter," said Dorian. "Not yet, anyway. This is something we need to ask an authority."

"Such as?"

"Aphrodite."

"Pardon?"

***

"Dorian Grey. Now aren't you a sight for sore eyes."

"You have Aphrodite on speed-dial?"

"What does that mean?"

"Some of us have tried to keep up with cultural norms, Dorian!"

"Yes, and that cultural norm is at *least* a decade out of date,

Robert."

"Boys, boys," said Aphrodite mildly. "Let's not bicker. You know I hate a lover's quarrel."

Aphrodite was the most beautiful woman either of them had ever seen. And she looked completely different to each of them; to Dorian, she resembled Dahlia, and to Robert, she looked like Desdemona.

"Ah, and you *are* lovers!" she rejoiced, clapping her hands together. "You know, humans these days, they mostly write erotica. No real *romances* I can sink my teeth into."

"I'm fairly certain they still write romances."

"*Robert Burns*," she said. "Now, this is a delight. Oh, I don't mean those dime-store novels, my dear. I mean real-life romances. Those are the stories I care about. These days, it's all fast-food love."

"Aphrodite," said Dorian, bowing. "Thank you for answering my summons."

"Anytime, pet," she said, smiling. "What is it to be today? What can I do for you, my little hedonist?"

Robert gaped at Dorian, who coughed delicately into his fist.

"Pardon, your worship, but I am not here on my own account," he said. "Well. Not in that way, anyhow."

Aphrodite sat back.

"Hm," she said. "How *disappointing*. And here I thought you'd brought me a gift."

She gave Robert a look that made *him* uncomfortable, which was a feat worth witnessing, although it may have been more because she resembled Desdemona in his eyes.

"Something has changed," Dorian pressed on. "Our stories, as it were."

Aphrodite tilted her head, as if she were considering something in the air.

"Yes," she agreed. "Something has changed. A little. A hairline fracture, as it were."

"And we'd like to know if it's," Dorian began, and then hesitated.

Aphrodite raised an eyebrow.

"He wants to know if it's real," Robert filled in. "As if he can't tell."

The goddess sighed and nodded.

"Yes, I remember you selkies were always a melancholy bunch," she said. "But Dorian – no. This is real. This, *hairline fracture*, shift of story, whatever you'd like to call it."

Dorian's eyes were huge, and he swallowed visibly.

"Is it so terrifying as all that?" she asked kindly. "Love?"

Dorian shook his head.

"Not love," he said.

"*New* love, then," she surmised. His brief nod told her everything she needed to know. "Well, my friend. It's what humans deal with every day, just as your poet said. Your story may have been a curse, but it was also a form of protection. Your armour, such as it was, is gone now."

"But...*him*?" said Dorian, looking at Robert. "It's so...*tacky.*"

"Thanks, Dorian," said Robert, rolling his eyes.

Aphrodite smiled.

"I have other responsibilities to attend to," she said. "But it may warm you, or not, to know you aren't the first. Not even the first of your kind, in fact, to have a different kind of story."

Dorian thought for a moment, then realisation hit.

"Iain," he said. Aphrodite nodded. "Lieutenant General Iain Grey, the selkie who couldn't love."

"And you were brothers in arms, after a fashion," said Aphrodite. "The world is changing, Dorian Grey. All we can do is change with it. Farewell."

Her mouth quirked up in a knowing smile.

"And, just by the by, there's nothing wrong with a little erotica," she said, before vanishing into the ether.

Dorian stood motionless, staring at the place Aphrodite had been.

Robert came up behind him, wrapping his arms around the selkie.

"Well," he murmured against Dorian's ear. "It seems this is as natural as breathing, Dorian."

The selkie was frozen in place. Terror was written across his features. Robert spun him around and kissed him soundly.

He blinked, uncertain and more terrified than he had ever been.

"Let's go get something to eat, shall we?" asked Robert, and led the reluctant selkie away.

***

"This *can't* be real."

"Why not?"

"Because I don't deserve it, Robert! I deserve to suffer."

They were at Fouquet's, chosen by Robert because he *always felt for the man, you know.* Dorian pointed out that this Fouquet was unrelated to Nicolas Fouquet, but Robert had insisted anyway.

"Our existence is suffering!" Robert was saying. "This is our chance, Dorian. Terrible things happen to people every day. People do bad things every day! Everyone has the right to redemption."

"Do you really believe that?"

"I've always believed it," said Robert. "Otherwise, how could I go on?"

"I didn't tell anyone what Magnus did," said Dorian. "Am I worth anything? Am I worth Leah's friendship, or the attentions of a man whose love was so fickle he fell in love with everything that moved?"

"Now that's unfair," said Robert. "I love Desdemona to distraction. You know that."

"Yes, and you were perfectly fine with using women in the meantime," snarled Dorian.

"You are crueller than you need to be," said Robert. "May I remind you that you lied to me for years about Des, not just Magnus."

"Exactly," said Dorian. "I don't deserve any of this!"

"Then become the kind of man who deserves it!" said Robert. "Nothing is written in stone, Dorian! Not even our stories! We thought they were. Now's our chance to be better men. Both of us. Stop trying to punish yourself! Stop running away from yourself and stop running away from me!"

Robert sighed, pushing his hands through his hair absent-mindedly.

"I don't understand why you're being so stubborn," he said.

"It's easy for you," said Dorian. "You, the great poet, with the adventurous life. You turned your hand to many things. What did I do? I was an indolent, drug-addled, spoiled, rich waste of time. I never even had an occupation! I don't see what you could possibly see in me."

Robert shook his head.

"I see the man who stood by his brother for years," he said. "I see the man who tried to shield me from pain. I see the man who is Leah Bishop's best friend. There's a reason you work at Interpol, Dorian, and it's not just because of history. It's who you are, beneath that stitched-up exterior. You love, deep as I do."

CHAPTER SEVEN

Lies and Other Truths

Maybe she was lying."

Robert dropped his fork onto his plate and leaned forward on his hands.

"Yes, the Greek goddess of love and beauty was *lying* to you," he said, sarcasm dripping off his words. "Face it, Dorian, she was after a roll in the hay with you or both of us. I doubt she would waste her time lying."

"But this *can't* be true!" Dorian insisted.

"I've had enough of this," said Robert. "What is so wrong with us finding love together all these years later, anyway?!"

"Because I still love Aidan and Dahlia, and it just seems *wrong*," Dorian hissed. "Disrespectful to their memories!"

"And I still love Desdemona with everything I am," said Robert. "That changes nothing about how I feel for you. Dorian, it's *hope*. Why don't you want it?"

Then he looked down at his plate.

"Oh," he said. "It's that you don't want *me*. Or you don't like that you've fallen for me. *Tacky*, isn't that what you said? Believe me, I know *exactly* the kind of man I was, Dorian, and I loved *every single person I was ever with!*"

Dorian stared at him in disbelief.

"So it's really true," he said. "You weren't just a hedonist."

"Not like you, apparently," Robert shot back. "I fell in love too easily. I hurt too easily! I am finding it in myself again, Dorian, and do you know what? This part of me is the *best* of me, and I think it's the best part of you, too! Empathy is what made Leah your best friend. It's what made you keep secrets. And why are you so surprised it could lead you to fall in love again, with someone you've known for hundreds of years?"

Robert dropped his napkin on his plate.

"I know who I am, selkie," he said. "Your arrogant demeanour, looking down on others, is the worst of you. It's the part that made Leah walk away. Now you have to decide: who you are, and more importantly, who do you want to be?"

"Robert –"

"No," he said. "I am going for a walk. I suggest you do the same. Think about what you're so afraid of, Dorian Grey, and whether the loss is worth the sacrifice."

He walked out of the restaurant, leaving Dorian with the bill.

Dorian had to admit it served him right.

***

There's nothing inherently lesser about happy endings.

There's nothing less literary about joy. Peace. Love. The positive things.

Dorian stared into the Seine, deep in thought.

About who he was. About what he wanted.

He'd never had to think about these things before.

At least, not for centuries.

And now, unbidden and terrifying, a leviathan from out of the deep –

An opportunity for change.

An opportunity *to* change.

Was he just more comfortable wearing these clothes of sorrow and ancient despair?

Was it because Robert was probably the most famous slut in all of Scottish history, and Dorian feared a broken heart?

In the end, the selkie had to admit that he, too, had such a history. It was only because he did not share Robert's fame that it was less well-known.

Arrogance. A downfall of Dorian's. He couldn't let go of Empire, much like many British people; and stuck in the Victorian era, the Victorian mores, the Victorian mindset, had given him an almost-permanent attitude of superiority.

But we've seen where that brought Britain, Dorian mused.

And it was nowhere good.

Here's your chance to become another kind of man.

Here's your chance to redeem yourself to Leah.

If she'll even believe this is happening.

Dorian smiled to himself when he thought of the running commentary he would have to endure from Leah, once all this got out.

That is, if she deigns to speak to me again.

I would understand if she couldn't.

I really would.

And that, there –

whatever had changed him, whatever had changed Robert, whether it was Leah or extended contact with humanity or a break in the fabric of reality, like Sebastian's spell on Burns Night, or like Sebastian's ability to break out of his own story –

or like Iain, the selkie who famously did not follow the rules.

Not out of intent, but simply *because* –

That was enough, to give him the little push toward acceptance.

Because it meant he could change. It meant he might get Leah back.

And above all, it meant he could legitimately be forgiven.

Maybe he could begin by forgiving other people, too.

***

The last of the sun was fading from the apartments as Dorian opened the door to see Robert silhouetted in a chair reading a book.

"Shouldn't be so near the window," said Dorian quietly. "It's dangerous."

Robert looked up with a soft smile, softened further by the play of golden light from the late afternoon sun.

"Desdemona taught me how," he explained. "She said it wasn't worth missing the sunsets or sunrises, not really. The most beautiful parts of the day. She taught me how to do it safely. She said a poet shouldn't miss it."

Dorian smiled.

"I never really knew what you saw in her," he said. "I think I am beginning to understand."

Robert nodded, closing the book, and standing up.

"She's incredible," he said.

He took Dorian's hand.

"As are you."

"Robert," said Dorian, so quietly Robert might not have heard him if it hadn't been recognisable as his own name.

"Dorian?" prompted Robert.

Full of fear, he looked up into Robert's strange, whisky-coloured eyes.

"If you're willing," he said. "I'd like to try."

The brilliant smile that crossed Robert's face put the setting sun to shame.

"I only awaited your word," he said, and captured Dorian's lips in a claiming kiss.

"I did have one question," said Robert.

"Which is?"

Dorian could feel him smile against his lips.

"Would you mind showing me some of that hedonism Aphrodite talked about?" he asked. "I know it's been years since you've been Taken."

Dorian could only smile in return.

"You never really forget."

CHAPTER EIGHT

Hedonism

I have to say," Dorian told Robert, who was panting, eyes wide, "I never expected you to be such a *giving* lover."

Suspended mid-air, Robert didn't answer.

Sweat trickled down his forehead, sliding off the tip of his nose.

He gasped, as Dorian slid the leather handle along his heated skin.

Dorian smiled.

***

Later, Dorian was seated in a chair, reading a book.

One of Robert's, as it happened.

Wordless, Robert walked into the living room.

With a single look from Dorian, he went to his knees.

Dorian ran a hand through Robert's hair as the poet leaned against him, staring up at him with something akin to awe in those amber-whisky eyes.

Submissive, thought Dorian. *Perfectly.*

Then again, he does love Desdemona.

So perhaps not quite a surprise.

His hand tightened in Robert's hair, earning him a soft moan.

Dorian smiled again.

***

The next few days were filled with curse words that Dorian extracted from Robert.

Pleasure. Pain. All the same.

*And he's so **pliant.***

Dorian told him so.

Robert basked in the praise.

***

Exhausted, Robert had fallen asleep, his head in Dorian's lap as the selkie read another book.

He'd allow it, for now.

When he woke, Dorian fed him pieces of pastry with a fork.

He shivered, watching Robert's tongue wrap around the silver tines.

Perhaps ... this isn't such a bad idea, thought Dorian Grey.

Now, looking down at Robert, whose wrists were held together behind his back, staring up at him with those enormous, trusting eyes, Dorian felt a little like his old self again.

Dorian observed this man who was willing to serve in any way he could, who was so open and ready for anything, and wondered if he had sorely misjudged him.

There it is again, that feeling.

My heart.

And if Robert Burns is the only vampire with a beating heart –
I wonder, sometimes, if I am the only selkie without one.

Dorian reached out and caressed Robert's cheek. The poet eagerly laid his head in Dorian's hand, clearly more interested in the future than the past.

Dorian shook his head.

So this was the man they all loved, he thought.

I see.

I see.

I see.

***

Later, before the sun had come up and Dorian had used all the creativity in his centuries-old arsenal, and Robert was adrift on exhaustion and satiety, the selkie went to stand in the balcony and watch the first tendrils of the dawn.

It's the past that brought us together.

It's the past that has kept us apart.

Perhaps Robert is correct, and we must all now look to the future.

We've navel-gazed and focused on history for so long, it's as if we have turned our back on these possibilities, these endless delights that might bring us a renewed happiness after all these years.

Life should not be a prison. We have served our time.

Dorian sighed. The pink and gold of dawn at the edge of the world gave way to the first rays of the rising sun.

He thought of Louis XIV, of the revolution, of the riots and the history of this city echoing down through the years.

And the love – what the city was famous for, all over the world.

Love symbolised hope. Hope for the future, rising from the ashes of the past.

He took a deep breath.

Perhaps there was something of the phoenix in them, too.

Dorian turned away from the beautiful morning sunrise and went to wrap himself around his lover, warm and safe.

Perhaps it had started as erotica.

But somewhere halfway along, it had become a story about love.

CHAPTER NINE

Scotland Calling

Dorian became aware of the world slowly and wondered what had woken him.

At his slight movement, Robert clung to him. The man was like an octopus.

Buzz-buzz.

Dorian opened his eyes and tried to reach his mobile from his position, which was impossible.

"Robert," he said gently. "I need to check the phone."

Robert grumbled and somehow wound himself even tighter around Dorian.

"*Robert*," said Dorian sternly, and Robert blinked awake. "Phone."

"Mmm," said Robert, "Okay."

He rolled over and stood up, giving Dorian an excellent view as he stretched.

Red welts stood out against unnaturally-pale skin, and Dorian felt oddly proud he had put those there.

"Show-off," said Dorian.

Robert just winked over his shoulder and went out to the kitchen.

Dorian grabbed the phone from the side table and was startled to see a message from Leah there.

"*That thing I told you about with Aoife's daughter has developed*," it said. "*Need you back here ASAP.*"

Dorian smiled, something painful in his heart easing.

It isn't everything, but it's a start.

Looking toward the future. No more living in the past.

"*Will find flights today, back soon,*" Dorian fired off.

He got up and walked into the kitchen, where he found Robert preparing some kind of fish breakfast.

"I think I'm in love," said Dorian.

The two men looked at each other, frozen in that moment.

"I mean," said Dorian, "Er –"

Robert gathered him up in his arms and kissed him soundly.

"It means whatever you want it to mean," he said. "Breakfast?"

"Absolutely," said Dorian.

"I do cook at the Angel's Share, you know," said Robert. "You always did like my fish."

"Indeed."

"Any news?"

"Oh," said Dorian, surprised he had already forgotten. "It's Leah. She's having trouble with a case and wants me to come back to Glasgow."

Robert's smile was brilliant.

"See?" he asked.

"I don't think it's a guarantee that things will go back to the way they were," said Dorian.

"Right," said Robert. "They might be even better."

"Optimist."

"Hedonist."

"It'll be our secret."

"Not with Leah involved. Not for long."

***

Travel to Glasgow from Paris was common, so they were able to pick up a flight in the evening long past sunset that would get them back to the city within the day.

As Dorian turned with his case to leave the Paris apartments again, he said a silent farewell to the place.

See you next century, he thought. *Maybe I'll be able to make it back sooner, next time.*

I've got a different kind of life ahead of me, after all.

The lock turned in the door, and the apartments faded into shadow, just as they had for hundreds of years, thousands of stories, and all the history held between their walls.

***

Dorian walked out into the arrivals hall of Glasgow International Airport.

Leah was standing there waiting, trying to hold back a grin.

"Miss Bishop," he said with a nod, secretly thrilled to see her.

"That's *Detective* to you, seal-man," she said.

"My apologies," said Dorian, bowing. "*Detective Inspector.*"

"That's better," she said. "How was the fli – *oof!*"

Dorian had thrown himself into her arms.

"What can I say?" he murmured into her shoulder. "I was homesick. Terribly so."

After a moment of startled silence, Leah's arms encircled him, too.

***

Robert emerged just then with the luggage, all smiles.

Leah raised an eyebrow.

"What's gotten into him?" she asked Dorian, as she went out to flag down a cab.

She turned around to see Robert shyly take Dorian's hand.

Leah's jaw dropped.

Her eyes nearly fell out of her head.

"You!" she said, pointing at Robert.

Then her eyes narrowed.

"*YOU!?*" she said, pointing at Dorian, and there was a *universe* of questions in the word.

"All in good time, Detective Inspector," said Dorian with a slight smile. "All in good time."

They climbed into the cab together, Leah folding down one of the seats and sitting facing away from the driver, ostensibly so she could keep an eye on them.

"I expect a full report, Dorian Grey," she said sternly.

"That's *Detective Inspector* to you," said Dorian primly.

Leah kicked him.

Dorian's smile would have put paid to the sun.

CHAPTER TEN

New Beginnings

The news was broken at Interpol, with all the usual suspects in attendance.

It was quite the development, after all: the announcement that here was obvious evidence things could change. For all of them.

There was hope.

"Oh my God," said Desdemona, her green eyes flashing bright. "Does this mean I'm free –"

"Oh, no," Robert assured her, his voice going syrupy-sweet. "I will *always* love you, Des. More than life itself. More than breathing."

"Great," said Desdemona flatly. "Fantastic."

"Oh! Can't you hear the birds singing??!!" Nour sang.

"I can hear *you* singing," said Desdemona.

Nour reached over and wrapped Desdemona's head in a scarf.

"*Wedding bells, with chirping birds,*" Nour said, her eyes fluttering shut. "Can't you just imagine it?"

"I can imagine a lot of things," said Desdemona. "Featherbrain."

"Oh, come now, you *must* love weddings!" trilled Nour.

"Remind me why we're friends again?" said Desdemona.

Robert was staring at her with big, soppy eyes.

She gave a loud, long sigh.

"Well, I'll give him one thing," she said. "He's consistent."

"All right, all right, break it up now," grumbled Chief Ben. "This is a cop show, not a soap opera."

Everyone noticed, however, that Ben kept the single red rose Robert had given him in a crystal vase on his desk and made sure it was watered.

"I wonder if the Chief will ever have a Valentine," mused Leah, as Dorian came to sit next to her on the sofa and their laptops curled up at their feet. The fire roared in the fireplace, just as it always had, and the firedogs slept there likewise.

"Anything is possible," said Dorian. "Now, Detective Inspector. Are you ready to fill me in?"

Leah nodded and went on to discuss the facts of the case.

Dorian smiled. He knew Interpol had always looked this way. He'd been working there a long time.

But it was better now, with the strong profile of Leah Bishop seated next to him on the sofa.

And that made all the difference.

CHAPTER ONE

The Great Hall of Caledonia Interpol was quiet and warm.

Cosy and welcoming, as always.

Detective Inspector Leah Bishop sipped her tea as she sat in front of the roaring fire. She was watching her partner, Dorian Grey, out of the corner of her eye, so he didn't suspect she was looking.

This was a fragile thing.

So many things were fragile, these days.

"So…how's it going?" asked Leah, setting her tea down on the table.

"I assume you are alluding to my recent dalliance with the vampire."

"Hmm," said Leah. "I didn't know you could blush."

Dorian pursed his lips.

"I am unsure whether he and I – whether we were capable of it," said Dorian.

"I'm pretty damned sure you're both capable of love."

"But of moving on?"

Leah nodded.

"And with each other," she said. "You haven't exactly been kind to vampires in the past. And I thought Taken selkies couldn't fall in love again. Selkie nature and all that."

"Not nature, as we previously believed, but law," said Dorian. "I thought the same, once upon a time."

"But you know as well as I do that laws can be broken."

"One of the many benefits of working in law enforcement."

"And here you thought your love story was –"

Here, Leah grinned large.

Dorian gave her a flatfaced look that had often sent her into gales of laughter in the past.

"Do not."

"Oh, I'm gonna."

"Very well. Proceed."

"*Sealed.*"

Dorian rolled his eyes and leaned forward on his cane.

"Feel better now? Was it all that you hoped?"

"It was pretty good, yeah."

Clouds moved across the ceiling, soft and fluffy. Today the weather was decent, at least.

"So, love. You think?"

"Too early to tell."

"Desdemona will be relieved, if it works out."

"I'm sure she would find it just as puzzling as his obsessive love for her over the centuries," said Dorian.

"Yeah, well. Something that doesn't experience human emotions is gonna be confused. Sometimes I think she's got it better than any of us. Emotions are a mess," said Leah. "But she's mentioned that Robert had other lovers over the centuries. Maybe he's not as single-minded as we thought."

"He was wed to Jeannie during the early years," agreed Dorian. "He often said she deserved better."

"He was right," said Leah.

Robert was a man for whom love was a perpetual fountain. But Desdemona would always be the central star of his heart. Even now, she was sure that had not changed. He had often assured Leah it never would.

And yet, he too had found solace in this tentative thing with Dorian.

Leah picked up her mug and took another sip of her tea.

Fragile, this thing between the two of them.

But for the first time, a symbol of hope –

the possibility that the Fae could change.

And change their own stories, without human interference or magic; that the Fae were not set in their ways like a carnival ride destined to follow the same curving path in perpetuity.

Which, of course, led her to consider the fragility of their own partnership.

Dorian and Leah were fast friends, once.

Best friends, she might have said.

But Dorian's hubris, his belief he was always in the right, and in the end, the things he had hidden from her, and from everyone –

meant their friendship had sustained a deep fracture.

Strange, Leah thought, how the poets and writers told so many stories of lost loves and breakups and divorces.

Very few of them discussed the heartbreak of losing a friend.

"Now, then," said Dorian, interrupting her reverie as he set his cane aside in the umbrella stand next to the sofa. "Enough about my dalliances. I believe you recalled me from Paris because you had something to discuss."

"Yeah," said Leah. "Remember before you left, we talked about kids reporting that the 'vampire with iron teeth' had returned to the Necropolis?"

"Yes, but we had concluded those stories were unsubstantiated," said Dorian. "There were no reports of missing children, in either human or monster law enforcement. Children have wild imaginations."

"They do," said Leah, "but in this case, I think the children may be right. Or at least they're seeing *something*. How many terrible things have happened because adults didn't believe kids, just because they had wild imaginations?"

Dorian nodded.

"I take your point."

"So while you were out on your lost weekend with Robert, I did a little digging."

"Literally?"

Leah smiled.

"No, I didn't go digging up graves," said Leah. "But I did talk to someone who seems to know more than we do."

"Indeed?" asked Dorian. "Who was that?"

"You're not going to believe this."

***

Caoimhe sat in the centre of the tea-party, not like a child, but like a god.

She smiled down at the teddy bears sitting around the table in the chairs, a benevolent but terrible ruler.

Caoimhe was a rarity. The child of an Irish goddess and a human man.

Aoife, the receptionist at Caledonia Interpol, and a warrior goddess of untold power, had given birth to the first demi-goddess in centuries.

"Welcome," Caoimhe said imperiously, as Dorian and Leah appeared in the doorway. "You may enter."

Dorian smiled, following Leah into the room.

"You may sit," said Caoimhe with a grand gesture.

"This child must be, what? Five years old?" said Dorian.

"Seven," said Caoimhe. "I can hear you."

Dorian inclined his head in acknowledgement.

"Caoimhe, I've brought Dorian here so you can tell him what you told me," said Leah. "About the vampire in the cemetery."

Caoimhe nodded, serious.

"It is a real problem," she said. "My subjects are concerned."

Dorian cast an eye at the teddy bears.

"Not them," said Caoimhe. "I just use them for practice. The other children."

"Your...friends?" hazarded Dorian.

Caoimhe stared at him.

"My *subjects*," she said, giving Leah a look that asked if he was stupid. "They are concerned about the monster. They tell me they've seen it snatching other children. Or at least that children are vanishing whenever it appears, which may not be quite the same thing, as you know."

"And you can't do anything about it."

"Sadly, my powers are weak," sighed Caoimhe. "Until I reach the age of majority, I will have to make do with what I have."

She held out her small arms and sighed again.

"Nevertheless," she said, "Mother tells me you two deal with these kinds of things, and you're the best of the best. I wouldn't want anything less for my subjects."

"Is that so."

"I am a good queen."

She held Dorian's gaze.

"Can you tell Dorian why you're certain the vampire stories are real?" asked Leah. "The same thing you told me?"

She nodded.

"The monsters under our beds," she said.

Dorian exchanged a look with Leah.

"That's where monsters come from, don't you know that?" said Caoimhe. "That's how they get out, and how you get in."

"You've been to Faerie?"

Caoimhe gave him a strange look and threw Leah a disbelieving *who is this guy* kind of expression.

"Once or twice. Mother doesn't like it, and she always says I can't go too far."

Caoimhe sighed, as if this were some great burden to bear.

"But Mother will not go to investigate. She says it's *not in her wheelhouse.* Leah's human so she can't go unless she's got someone supernatural with her, and I can't go myself because, well."

She looked at her arms again.

"However. I believe my subjects when they tell me children have been taken, whether or not it has been reported. I'd like you to investigate for me."

She gave Dorian a disdainful frown.

"I trust this meets with your satisfaction?"

"Yes, thank you, Caoimhe," said Leah. She elbowed Dorian.

"I thank you as well," he said, bowing deeply. This, at least, seemed to amuse her.

"Your words please me," she said. "You are dismissed."

***

"There is something wrong with that child."

Leah laughed as they walked together along the Clyde. It was a beautiful day, as Glasgow marks them, with bright sunlight and a light mist off the water. They had just gone to a curry house and were carrying warm polystyrene boxes that smelled delicious.

"She's just precocious. She's a demi-goddess. She'll grow out of it."

"Hopefully."

They sat down together on the banks of the river. Leah flipped open her box of tikka masala and speared a piece of chicken on her plastic fork. She took a bite and leaned back, making an *mmmm* sound.

"I don't care what they say about Edinburgh," she said. "Glasgow makes the best curry."

"Tikka masala was invented here, after all," said Dorian, primly opening his own box and delicately lifting his fork. "Yet my personal preference will always be for French cuisine."

Leah rolled her eyes good-naturedly.

"Not everyone can afford to be a snob, eating French fancies on the Seine with Robert Burns," said Leah.

"I assure you, we did more than that."

"Whoa! TMI!" Leah said, but then noticed the corners of his mouth curving upward, which on Dorian was a wide smile. "Oh, fuck you."

She flicked some rice at him with her fork. It missed by a mile.

He smoothed the front of his brocade vest.

"It's for the best," he said. "I only just got this drycleaned."

Leah laughed, and they just sat together, appreciating the decent weather, and eating in companionable silence.

"Leah –" Dorian began suddenly, and just by the tone of his voice, she knew where this was heading.

She froze, alarmed.

They had somehow avoided broaching the subject of their friendship back at Interpol. It almost felt like old times.

But Leah knew better.

"Can we not?" she asked. "I don't want to do this right now. Let's just. I don't know, appreciate the moment?"

❀ CHAPTER ONE ❀

Dorian's expression slammed shut in a way Leah had never seen before. She knew how difficult it was for him to be vulnerable in any way, and suddenly hated herself for what she'd said.

But he nodded, and looked out at the water, steadfastly complying with her request.

Leah thought she could kick herself, sometimes.

CHAPTER TWO

"So what's the plan?"

"Dorian and I will travel together," said Leah.

Chief Ben gave her a stern look.

"Is that altogether wise?"

"I live in a flat in Faerie, Chief," said Leah. "I think I'll be fine."

"You live in a flat in a particular *part* of Faerie," said Ben. "Not the Fae underworld! Just like the human world, there are better and worse places to be."

"Like Glasgow," said Leah cheerfully. Ben glowered.

"Are you calling my job into question, Detective?" he asked. She shrugged.

"Yours and mine."

Ben shook his head and handed her a stack of paperwork.

"Let me know how you get on," he said. "And ask Aoife if she'll bring me a black coffee, will you?"

"Sure thing, Chief," said Leah.

***

Leah met up with Dorian at the sofa in the Great Hall where they did most of their brainstorming.

She looked up and saw Aoife carrying a huge pot of what looked like black sludge. Leah grinned.

"Something amusing?" asked Dorian. He was expertly turned out in a dark purple Victorian waistcoat, which he straightened when he rose to greet her.

"The Chief's industrial-strength coffee," said Leah, sitting down. Dorian sat down at the same time, ever the gentleman.

There were two cups of tea sitting on the coffee table. She glanced at them.

Dorian cleared his throat.

"I took the liberty of making you tea," said Dorian. "Milk, no sugar. Yes?"

He looked strangely hopeful.

Something by way of an apology, thought Leah absently.

"Yeah," she said. Then she picked up the cup and saucer, both of which always seemed too delicate. "Thank you."

"No bother," said Dorian. He lifted his own cup and saucer, taking a sip as he hid his face, along with any emotion, behind the cup. "Now. Shall we discuss the case?"

"I have a couple of theories," said Leah. "One: time travel. The Fae live outside of time, right? So this vampire, if it *is* a vampire, coming in and out of the time periods when it gets caught? Twenty, fifty years, it won't be noticed. Two: the power of belief creates the monster, but I'm less certain on that one. It's kind of an American thing."

"Monsters work differently over there," Dorian agreed. "They are not so confined by story, but stories change there so quickly they have more ability to move."

"The other thought I had," said Leah, "was that children are more likely to see ghosts and monsters. That is an established fact."

Dorian nodded.

"Children and animals," he said.

"So do you think we might need Caoimhe?" asked Leah. "As a guide?"

"I don't like putting a child in such danger."

"Maybe not for the entire time," said Leah, "but I don't know if either of us will be able to access that part of Faerie on our own."

"Meaning that you think if we try to go under the bed –"

"There won't be a door open for us," finished Leah. "Fludge may have come from the same land of monsters, but I've never seen anything like a doorway or staircase under my bed."

"Then I think we need to ask Aoife if she'll let Caoimhe help us."

***

⚜ CHAPTER TWO ⚜

"Absolutely not."

"Aoife, this creature is attacking people who are fool enough to go into the Necropolis at night," Dorian tried reasoning with her.

"And you want to bring *my child* into that environment? *No.*"

Aoife wouldn't budge. She was a formidable receptionist, which was the absolute worst kind.

And the best.

Ben often said she was worth her weight in gold.

"I'm not letting you put Caoimhe in danger, Dorian Grey," Aoife said. Her arms were crossed, the outline of her muscles visible beneath her tattoos.

Although Aoife was an Irish warrior goddess, her centuries in Scotland meant she was as Scottish as any of them. Her blonde hair was up in a sprightly ponytail and the bright friendly colours of her vintage retro rockabilly dress seemed in contrast to her powerful nature.

"Mother. If I may."

Caoimhe stood there, crayons and paper behind her, where she had been drawing during her visit to the office.

"Caoimhe, I forbid it."

"They are working for me," Caoimhe informed her.

She turned to Leah and Dorian.

"What do you need?"

Leah looked from Aoife's stormy expression to Caoimhe's open, neutral one.

"You are *not* going to the underworld," said Aoife sternly.

"You go there every day to smoke!" Caoimhe retorted.

"I'm a grown goddess!" argued Aoife.

Caoimhe sighed.

"If I open the door and lead them in, and then come right back," she said, "will that be all right with you?"

Aoife gave Leah and Dorian an angry look.

"You do *not* want to piss off the receptionist," she reprimanded them. "There's no one else to look after her, and I need to work."

57

"Noted," said Dorian.

"We wouldn't be asking a child for help if there were any other way," said Leah. "None of us are young enough to gain access."

"I don't think it's entirely safe that children can gain access to the underworld," said Aoife.

"Mother, I'm a demigoddess," said Caoimhe. "I'll be fine."

Aoife knelt in front of her daughter.

"It is *exactly* because you're a demigoddess that your mother worries," said Aoife. "You are clever and strong, Caoimhe. But there are plenty of creatures and people who would kidnap a child like you and not think twice about it."

"Kidnap me?" asked Caoimhe. "Whatever for?"

"Ransom," said Dorian. "Murder, possibly. A dead demigoddess is worth quite a lot in the right circles –"

"*Dorian*," hissed Leah, looking into Caoimhe's big, round eyes. "*Stop. Helping.*"

"Apologies," said Dorian with a slight bow.

But his words seemed to have gotten through to Caoimhe, because she turned to her mother and said:

"I understand. I will open the door for them and go no further."

Aoife nodded, and then stood up.

"I apologise if my words were ill-considered, Aoife," said Dorian. "It was not my intention to frighten her."

"On the contrary," Aoife said. "You scared her straight. She's a powerful little girl. She can get ahead of herself. I remember when I was her age, and – well."

"We promise to close the door behind us," said Leah.

"How will you get back?" asked Aoife.

"Find the door where we first entered and knock, I presume," said Dorian. "If Caoimhe will be so kind as to let us in."

Caoimhe nodded gravely.

"A sentinel has an important job," she said. "It is one I will take seriously."

She nodded to Aoife.

"Farewell, Mother," she said.

Aoife kissed Caoimhe on the top of her head.

"I'll see you after work," she promised. Caoimhe nodded.

"Now, then," she said. "Shall we?"

***

Caoimhe's room still had remnants of her earlier tea party.

"Do your friends come over and have tea with you?" asked Leah.

Caoimhe gave her a look.

"I don't really have friends."

Leah found it interesting that she didn't mention her *subjects,* this time.

"Really?" asked Leah. "Why is that?"

"I don't know," Caoimhe sighed. "They think I'm strange. Different. Too strong."

"Kids can be mean."

"I don't think it's that," said Caoimhe. "I am the only one of my kind. They fear me."

"Oh," said Leah.

Dorian knelt to look her in the eye, much to Leah's surprise.

"Humans sometimes don't understand us," said Dorian. "It's not their fault. I often don't understand us, either. But they are good at the core."

Caoimhe gave him a look like she doubted him.

"If you say so," she said.

Then she went over to the bed and pushed it away from the wall.

"There," said Caoimhe. "Can you see it?"

Leah and Dorian stared at the wooden floor. Both shook their heads.

"I don't –" Leah began. "Wait!"

Sure enough, the wood seemed to deepen and darken.

Moments later, a staircase appeared, tight against brick walls leading down.

"There it is," said Caoimhe. "The staircase to the underworld."

CHAPTER THREE

"Well," said Leah. "No time like the present."

"There certainly is not," Dorian replied, leaning on his walking stick.

"Mother says I can't go any further," said Caoimhe.

"That's okay, Caoimhe, we can take it from here," said Leah. She turned to Dorian.

"Ready?"

"After you."

"Oh, no," said Leah, a knife edge to her smile. "I insist."

"Then together," Dorian suggested. "Side by side."

Leah nodded mutely. Caoimhe looked back and forth between them and shook her head.

"Grownups," she said.

Leah and Dorian stood at the precipice.

They stepped down onto the first stair leading to the darkness below.

Together.

***

"So. You live here now," said Dorian, awkwardly trying to start a conversation.

"In Faerie, yeah," said Leah. "I don't know why you don't. The weather sure is better."

Dorian laughed a little.

"In Glasgow, you have human concerns," said Dorian. "When all is said and done, those are the problems I prefer. Mould on the walls. Location. Whereas in Faerie, you have Fae problems. Sometimes your front door opens onto a waterpark. Sometimes it opens onto the night sky if it's feeling whimsical. Sometimes your house gets infested by squorbles."

"What are squorbles?" asked Leah.

"Your landlord didn't mention them?"

"No."

"Huh," said Dorian. "Then I take it we have slumlords in Faerie, too."

"Landlord's nice enough," said Leah. "Maybe he didn't think of it."

"Remind me, upon our return," said Dorian smoothly, "to have a word with him, won't you?"

"Sure."

They kept walking downward. The staircase seemed as if it would never end.

"These monsters must have a lot of problems getting up and down these stairs," said Leah. "Keeps 'em fit, I guess."

"Or it's an illusion."

"How do you mean?"

Dorian stopped still on the staircase. He rapped sharply against the wall with his cane. Then again, and then again in another place.

To Leah's surprise, the cane vanished into the wall.

"How'd you do that?" she asked.

"Illusion. See?"

And he walked through the wall and vanished.

"Hey!" shouted Leah, alarmed.

Dorian's head poked back through the wall.

"Follow me, Leah. It's perfectly safe."

Leah gave him a look. He rolled his eyes.

"Insofar as Faerie is safe," he said. "Come along."

Leah took a deep breath and followed Dorian through what looked like a solid wall –

into a bright, white room surrounded with long black sofas.

"What is it?" she asked. "Looks like a waiting room."

"Perhaps a kind of green room?" asked Dorian. "Wait here, then showtime?"

Leah nodded.

"Then do we wait, or keep going?"

"I think we keep going."

"I was afraid you were going to say that."

Dorian put his hand on the door handle and turned it.

They walked out –

into a market.

"Shit," said Dorian.

Leah wheeled around and stared at him in astonishment.

"Dorian Grey, are you feeling all right?"

Dorian coloured a bit, high and pink on his cheeks.

"I may have been spending too much time with Robert," he admitted.

"I have never heard you swear," she said.

"Indeed," said Dorian primly, adjusting his cufflinks. "It's unbecoming."

"Which means you had a reason," said Leah. "What's up?"

Dorian indicated the swirling world they found themselves a part of, with creatures of all shapes and varieties hawking their wares, haggling over prices, and music playing in the general cacophony of it all.

"This," said Dorian, in a voice tinged with despair. "The Goblin Market."

"Goblin Market?" asked Leah. "What, like that Christina Rossetti poem?"

"Yes," Dorian nodded. "Although it was...less creative license and more autobiographical, shall we say."

"So that means –"

"Don't eat the fruit."

Leah nodded, and they began to move through the Market.

Regardless of the danger, Leah was charmed. She'd studied folklore for so many years, including the poem they had discussed, and it never failed to amaze her that all those creatures were real. Here, they took their real forms, whereas those that lived topside in the human world often looked human. Leah mentioned as much to Dorian.

"Yes, it's a real problem," said Dorian. "Equal opportunity has not quite arrived at Interpol, and it's a common refrain. Then again, some creatures are considered beyond rehabilitation."

"No one is beyond rehabilitation," said Leah. "If you want to call it that."

"The term *Goblin Market* is something of a misnomer, anyway," said Dorian. "It's really the *Faerie Market*, but the name stuck. All the Fae come here to buy, sell, and trade. It's dangerous for humans, but it's no safe place for us either."

"Then why come here?" asked Leah. "Are there things the Fae need they can't get topside?"

"We aren't underground," said Dorian, "although I see why you might make that mistake. But in another sense, this is the Fae underworld. Not necessarily criminal, but a place for all variety of shady dealings."

"Lady," said a voice near their feet.

Leah looked down to see a small round creature.

"Pretty jewels for a pretty lady?"

It held out a handful of gemstones that sparkled in the light.

"No thank you," said Leah politely.

The small creature waddled onward and disappeared into the crowd.

"Good thing you turned him down," said Dorian. "Those things make your eyelashes fall out."

"What?" asked Leah, puzzled. "Why?"

Dorian shrugged.

"Rules of Fae are not the same," he said. "Someone apparently finds human eyelashes valuable. And we might not find other sellers to be quite so polite."

"Oh my God," said Leah, stopping dead in her tracks, as she recognised the layout among the hustle and bustle of the marketplace. "I *thought* this place looked familiar! It's the Barras. This is the *Fae Barras*."

"You would be correct," said Dorian. "As above, so below, as the Christians are so fond of saying. Keep in mind Aonghas did not always look like a Celtic football supporter. As the human world changes, so too does Faerie."

"Then does the map of Faerie mirror Glasgow?" asked Leah. "This part of it, at least? An underground world that follows the same streets and pathways?"

"I believe so," said Dorian. "I haven't been to this part of Faerie in a long time, so my memory of the area is imperfect, but if the Goblin Market has the same layout as the Barras, then the answer is most likely yes."

"Okay," said Leah. "Then I think we should stop wandering around aimlessly, hoping to find something, and we go directly to the source."

"The Necropolis?"

"Well, yes, eventually," said Leah. "But we need to question people first, and there aren't a lot of people in a cemetery."

"I think you'll find –"

"I mean *living* people," Leah interrupted. "Living Fae, at least."

"Questioning ghosts can often be helpful," Dorian suggested. "I've gotten many a lead from a spirit."

"Spirits of both kinds, I'd guess," Leah said, grinning. "But let's go find out what we can find out from the Fae in the bad parts of town."

CHAPTER FOUR

"Are we in *Bridgeton*?"

"Brigton," said Leah, with the local pronunciation. "And yeah. Where else?"

"I fail to see –"

"Cops – regular human cops – told me this was the absolute worst part of town these days," said Leah. "CCTV's been broken here for years, everybody knows it."

"How does that relate to the Fae underworld version of Glasgow?"

"As above, so below."

"Touché."

Leah and Dorian walked through the dimly-lit fog. If she didn't know where she was, she might have called it beautiful.

Since this was Glasgow, she called it beautiful anyway.

Glasgow was all about the magic in the mundane, and here, the mundane was magic.

"Can I help ye?" asked a voice out of the darkness.

They stopped. Dorian slid his hand around the head of his walking stick, subtly changing both its position and his posture.

A wizened old woman emerged from the fog. She seemed to be wearing it over her shoulders like a shawl or a blanket.

Dorian broke into a grin.

Since Leah didn't even think he knew what those were, she was instantly suspicious.

"*Cailleach*!" Dorian cried.

"Rude," Leah said.

The old woman peered at him. She pushed her bifocals up on her nose.

"Dorian?" she croaked shakily. "Bless my soul, is that young Dorian Grey I see?"

"Hello, Cailleach," said Dorian, warm as fresh bread. "How have you been keeping?"

"Same as ever, laddie, same as ever," said the old woman. "Who's this?"

"My partner at Interpol, Detective Inspector Leah Bishop," said Dorian.

The old woman peered up at her.

"You stick it to 'em, lassie!" she crowed. "Women's liberation is making leaps and bounds!"

Dorian leaned over.

"Her sense of time is a little –"

"But not my hearing," said the old woman. "I'm the Old Woman of Winter, or the *Cailleach*, but you can call me Beira."

"Beira," said Leah, and shook her hand, "I've heard of you."

"Fame at last," said Beira. "Now, where are the other handsome young seals? Off basking, I suppose."

"Most likely," Dorian agreed.

When Beira moved, Leah was enchanted to see that the fog spreading over her shoulder was a finely-woven tartan pattern.

"It nears time for the washing," said Beira. "Then the winter, as you know."

"Oh, you couldn't wait a while longer?" asked Dorian. "Leah does so love the summertime. Something to do with champagne and Pimm's in the park. I keep telling her it's illegal to drink alcohol in the park, she keeps telling me she's a police officer."

"Can't keep the seasons waiting, my lad," she said. "But I'll give you a long, warm autumn, if that's an acceptable compromise."

"Thank you," said Dorian. "That is very generous."

"Now, what brings you to these parts?" asked Beira. "These are dangerous streets, laddie."

"Yes, I know," said Dorian. "It was Leah's hunch, really."

"Then I shall ask her. Leah, lady detective, I shall never get over that! What is it you're looking for? Granny Beira might be able to help."

"Children have gone missing from the Necropolis," said Leah. "This is the second time now. The last time was in the

68

50s."

"I don't recall that tale told in the 1750s," said Beira.

"She means the 1950s," said Dorian.

Beira looked up at him.

"Has it been so long?" she asked. Dorian nodded.

"Well, then," said Beira. "There's nothing else for it. Would ye like to come round for a wee cuppa?"

"Here?" said Dorian. "I thought you lived in Dalmally, or thereabouts."

"Oh, silly lad," said Beira, waving her hand at him. "That's my *winter* home. I summer here."

"You summer," said Dorian, "in Bridgeton."

"That's *Brigton*," said Beira. "And yes, of course. Now, would you like some tea?"

"I'm dying for a cup," said Leah.

"You see?" said Beira. "Smart lass. Come along now."

And they followed Beira and her grey-tartan cloak of fog into the night.

***

Everything about Beira's flat was comfortable, quaint, and well-lived-in.

Leah sat on a sofa that seemed to be stuffed with a hundred lumpy pillows. A knit blanket was thrown over the back. There was a biscuit tin filled with sewing bits and bobs. A fire in the fireplace crackled soft and merry. An elderly Scottie dog blinked rheumy eyes up at Leah and waddled over to her, laying down over her feet with a contented sigh.

"That's Old Man Snorfles," Beira said. "He's a wee daftie, but I love him."

"I have a pet...creature...at home," said Leah. "His name is Fludge."

"That's nice, dear."

Beira handed her a milky tea in a chipped cup that said *World's Best Grandma!* and a floral china saucer. The old woman smiled kindly at her, and Leah saw that she'd put three choc-olate digestive biscuits on the saucer with the tea.

Beira shuffled around in her slippers, busying herself with serving Dorian. Then she sat down with her own cup and leaned back in her armchair with a satisfied sigh.

Leah thought she could fall asleep like this; the place was so comfortable and warm.

Like home, she thought, and had the sudden realisation that nothing had felt so much like *home* for years upon years.

"Now, then," said Beira. "Tell Granny all about it."

So Dorian explained the history of the vampire. Back in the 1950s, it was said to haunt the Necropolis, and children were being attacked. Children were also involved in fighting it off, although whether the vampire was real, or a myth based on the overpopularity of the comic books of the time, was never discovered."

"Brave little children," said Beira. "It's incredible, isn't it? What the fearlessness of childhood can do."

"And every vampire I know swears they've never met this vampire," Dorian finished, "or encountered a vampire with iron teeth anywhere."

"I thought it might have something to do with childlore," said Leah. "It's a branch of folkloric study, based on things children often do. Schoolyard songs, local kids' legends, things like that."

"A powerful child must have guided you here," said Beira. "After all, this is something of a place of nightmares."

"Yes, our receptionist Aoife, you recall?"

"Oh, yes, Aoife, how is she?" said Beira.

"Very well. She had a child, and as you know those children grow quickly."

"Another goddess?"

"A demigoddess. Human father," said Dorian. "He's *not in the picture*, as they say these days."

"Men," said Beira, and then patted him on the arm. "Sorry, dear."

"No offence taken," said Dorian. "He was, incidentally, killed by a vampire. But I must ask, what are *you* doing here? In a place of nightmares, as you say."

Beira smiled.

"Don't you know, laddie?" she asked. "That's the safest place you can be. Safe as houses."

Then she looked at Leah, who was struggling to keep her eyes open.

"And you say these disappearances have started again."

"Yes."

"Then I think I have the very thing."

CHAPTER FIVE

hatever it is, we'll give it a shot."

"Are you certain about that?" asked Beira.

Dorian and Leah exchanged glances.

"Shouldn't we know what we're agreeing to beforehand?" Leah asked Dorian.

"Seeing the world through a child's eyes," Beira said. "Now. Are you willing?"

Leah wasn't sure, but finally nodded.

"Yes," they agreed.

"Very well," said Beira, and sat back, sipping her tea.

A moment passed. Then another.

"Don't you need to…do a spell or something?" ventured Leah.

Beira laughed.

"Oh, no, my dear," she said. "That's for amateurs."

"I see."

The room was warm, and the fire crackled as Old Man Snorfles proved the reason for his name, smacking his lips together and giving voice to loud, snuffling snores.

Leah opened her eyes.

"Sorry!" she said, sitting up and yawning. "I must've fallen asleep."

"Don't you worry, dear," said Beira kindly. "You both deserved some rest."

The old woman seemed taller than she had been earlier.

Then Leah turned to Dorian, to tell him they should go.

And her voice died in her throat.

Seated beside her was a child of ten or twelve years, dressed in Dorian's impeccable Victorian style. He was asleep.

"Dorian!" hissed Leah.

Dorian blinked at the world around him.

"I must have dozed off," he said. "My apologies, Beira."

"As I told your companion," said Beira, "sometimes rest is needful."

Dorian turned to Leah and then shrank back in shock.

"Leah!" he said. "You're –"

"Right back at you," Leah replied.

Dorian turned to Beira and narrowed his eyes.

"What have you done?"

"I think your partner had the right idea," said Beira. "It's good we ran into each other, as I doubt you'd have found your way to the answer on your own."

"We're *children*!" exclaimed Leah.

"Of course, dear, but only for the moment," Beira reassured her. "Children and animals can see monsters the rest of us cannot. I am an old woman, and magic or not, I am less likely to be of any assistance in the matter. So, if we cannot put real children in danger, this is the second-best thing – and the best chance we have to find out if the monster is real."

"Beira, we cannot go about the city like this!"

"And why not?" she asked. "Even in Faerie, children are charmed things. People pay less attention to children running around, whether here or in the mundane world."

"But I can't be a police officer!" said Leah.

"Don't worry too much, dear," said Beira. "It will wear off in a few hours. After that, you can both go back to your lives. But this may be your best opportunity to see what children see. You may catch the monster in action, if there is a monster to catch."

Dorian sighed in resignation. He nudged Leah with his elbow, and she gave him an angry look but maintained her silence.

"Thank you, Beira," he said.

"Anytime, young man," she said. "Now, you'd best be on your way. Magic only works for a brief spell. Things always want to go back to the way they truly are, so you're working against the clock."

"All right," said Dorian. "Leah?"

Leah, still discomfited, hopped off the sofa and followed

Dorian outside into the darkness, as Old Man Snorfles trailed them to the door.

"Be safe!" called Beira after them, and then shut the door against the chill of the Glasgow night.

Darkness folded around them, both familiar and new.

Leah rounded on him once they were alone outside Beira's house.

"*Dorian.*"

"I know," Dorian held up a hand as he tried to placate Leah. "But she means well, and she may well be right. We were willing to put Caoimhe in harm's way, after all."

Leah counted to ten in her head. Then she did it again for good measure.

"Then let's get to the Necropolis," she said, "and find out what's really going on, before we lose the ability."

The walk to the Necropolis was a long one, and now even longer because their legs were shorter.

Leah wasn't exactly certain of the reason, but a lot of the things that had concerned her just hours before had melted away.

Now, she was on an adventure with her best friend. Their recent arguments and fights seemed ridiculous and far away and grown-up.

"Wow," she said, pointing up at the orange-purple bruised sky of a late-summer Glaswegian evening. "Look at that!"

"It's beautiful."

"Do you think it's aliens?"

"No," said Dorian. "Aliens aren't real."

"Well, if *you're* real, and you aren't supposed to be real, then how do you know for sure?" asked Leah.

"Good point."

Somewhere along the way, Leah found an interesting stick. Dorian's walking stick also became more useful, whether for duelling or using as a bat, as children do. The two friends kept pausing to investigate various things: a frog at the side of the road; a little shelter someone had carved out for themselves in the city; strange gargoyles with mysterious and cryptic messages, their faces eroded away with weather and time.

The world seemed to teem with possibility.

"When I was a kid," said Leah, "everything seemed magical. Just, the whole world seemed gigantic and full of *potential*, you know? Adventure."

She sighed.

"Growing up sucks," she said with feeling.

"I hardly remember my childhood," admitted Dorian. "Mostly it was spent in the sea, playing with the other selkies, and my brother Magnus."

He grimaced. Magnus had always been a sensitive subject, even moreso of late.

"You know," said Leah, "We used to just have fun for the sake of it. No booze, no worries."

"Indeed," said Dorian.

"We better pick up the pace," said Leah. "The Necropolis is still far away."

So they did, and as they walked, they found delight and joy in all the little things on the way. Some were distracting, some were just silly conversations about unlikely events.

"But if your *hand* was cut off by a falling chandelier –"

"That's ridiculous, you'd have more to worry about than just your *hand* if the chandelier fell –"

"What if it was a *magic* chandelier –"

"Well, that's unfair because there are all kinds of different magic, I'm talking about, like, a *regular* chandelier –"

"I think it would hurt either way –"

and other such nonsense, Leah found she was genuinely enjoying herself for the first time in an awfully long time.

"There it is!" said Dorian, in a reverent voice, as he pointed at a hill they had seen and traversed many times.

The great silhouette of the Necropolis loomed ahead.

But now, it felt like the goal at the end of a daring journey.

***

The Glaswegian city of the dead spreads its great shadow over the town.

Many people went there for picnics or to take moody photographs, since its views over Glasgow were unmatched. It was the final resting place of all the great and the good. The towering Glasgow Cathedral was dwarfed by the Necropolis, and was the burial place of Mungo, Glasgow's patron saint. There were no places that could be called more essentially Glaswegian than either of these: the cathedral, and the city of the dead.

"What do you think we'll find up there?" asked Leah, as they sneaked through the hole in the fence along the side of the road, which was the same in Faerie as it was in the city itself.

"I don't know," said Dorian. "But it will probably be surprisingly Glaswegian."

Leah laughed, because this was the most hilarious thing she had ever heard.

77

CHAPTER SIX

s it happened, when they reached the top of the hill, the Necropolis was quite crowded.

There seemed to be some kind of an event going on, and a lot of people were in attendance.

"Now, then," said a man who was the current speaker. "What do we think about Scottish independence? It is looking more likely by the day."

"Foolish!" called out one woman.

"About time!" called out a man.

"Disgraceful!" said someone else.

An argument ensued among the people gathered there.

"What's going on?" whispered Leah.

Dorian studied the crowd.

"It appears to be," he said slowly, "a ghost conference."

"Ghosts have conferences?"

"The Necropolis is a special place," said Dorian. "Here, in Faerie, *city of the dead* takes quite the literal meaning. They are holding a town hall, of sorts."

"What do you –" Leah began, but then noticed all around them, superimposed in a ghostly white, were buildings of various types. She could dimly read the outlines of various store names and realised they were standing in a shopping district complete with mall and curry house and bookies.

"What do ghosts bet on?" she asked. "What do ghosts bet *with*?"

"I'm afraid you probably wouldn't like the answer," said Dorian.

He paused, and then clarified:

"Either answer."

They suddenly became aware that the ghost convocation had fallen silent.

"Er," said Leah, as she stared back at all the ghosts staring at her with their gaping mouths and strange eyes.

"A human child," said one of them, floating closer. "What is a human child doing here?"

"Forget the human child," said another. "What about this seal-pup? Have you gone astray, seal-pup? So far from the sea."

"I read that you'll find seals in all sorts of strange places," said one ghost. "In houses, in rivers. I saw one in a restaurant booth, once."

"You don't find seals at the top of the Necropolis, I wouldn't imagine," sniffed the first ghost.

"Seals could find their way to such places," said the other loftily. "I saw one on the news. It was on the top of a building."

"Now that's a fib if I ever heard one!" said the first ghost.

"Are you calling me a *liar* –"

"Please, gentlemen!" said Dorian, in his tiny voice that nevertheless rang with its Victorian gravity. "We have come to investigate stories about the vampire with iron teeth. Do you know it?"

"*Iron*," repeated one of the ghosts in terror. "What iron?"

"Oh, I know what he's talking about!" said the other ghost, who was fond of seals, in a smug voice. "The great menace to the children of Glasgow, you recall it? In the 50s."

"I don't pay attention to these new-fangled stories," sniffed the first ghost, and floated back to the conversation about Scottish independence, which had started up again.

"Don't pay attention to him, seal-pup and human child," said the ghost. "He doesn't know anything. He thinks the Industrial Revolution was the height of technology."

"And you don't."

"I am very modern," said the ghost proudly, "I use the *Internet*."

"Oh," said Dorian, feigning polite interest, because it was the done thing.

"*How?*" asked Leah.

"Yes," said the ghost proudly, not gracing Leah with a satisfying answer. "Although I cannot seem to get the video chats to work, and the machine keeps mysteriously downloading – er, let's just say, *questionable material* – all by itself. Although that has also been, shall we say, educational. A learning experience. I like to keep myself informed."

"A moment, if you will?" asked Dorian politely. The ghost nodded, and Leah took Dorian aside.

"This is what we've got to go on?" asked Leah. "A ghost that has the technological aptitude of somebody's gran on a Skype call?"

"If we weren't children right now, we might never have seen any of them," Dorian reminded her. "We're detectives, we go on hunches all the time. This is our glimpse behind the veil."

"Couldn't we ask Hazel?"

"Hazel's just a ghost," said Dorian. "Ghostly status doesn't confer knowledge on its own. She has little connection to the underworld, especially nowadays, working at the lab with Milo. Besides, this ghost has been here the entire time. If something has happened, he'll have seen it."

They returned to the ghost, which had been floating politely some distance away.

"We would appreciate it if you could help us," said Dorian. "We are detectives from Caledonia Interpol."

The ghost gasped.

"They're recruiting awfully young these days," he said. Then its eyes grew wide. "I didn't do anything illegal, officers – I don't think?"

"Don't worry about that," said Leah. "We're here about the vampire and the vampire only."

The ghost breathed a sigh of relief.

"See something, say something," he said proudly. "I am a responsible citizen of Glasgow."

"Aren't you dead?" asked Leah. The ghost gave her a surprised look.

"Still a citizen," he said.

"As Billy Connolly said, Glasgow doesn't care much for the living, but really looks after the dead," Leah told Dorian under her breath.

"My name is Charles Tennant," said the ghost. "I have always been active in Scotland's future. Look ahead, never behind, that's my motto."

"Charles Tennant?" said Leah, surprised. "The railway tycoon?"

"And many other things," he said. "Social reform has always been important to me. Some of these people, well, they argue for argument's sake. I wanted to make a change, make Scotland a powerhouse. I may be a ghost now – imagine my surprise at that! – but I still take a keen interest in the future of the nation. Perhaps Scotland is my unfinished business."

"And in your time here, have you noticed anything strange?" asked Dorian. He cast an eye at the ghost convocation, now arguing about Gregg's vegan sausage rolls. "Stranger than usual, that is."

"Well, I don't know about any vampires," said Charles. "But I can say that the children of *my* time used to refer to trains as monsters with iron teeth."

"Trains?" asked Leah, confused. "Because of the cow-catchers on the front?"

"Yes," Charles agreed. "So if that was the case then, it stands to reason that children without the language to describe something they are seeing might come up with a new description entirely."

"Then what would children today describe as a *vampire with iron teeth?*" wondered Leah.

The ghost shrugged, which was a strange thing to see.

"You're today's children," said Charles. "You tell me."

Leah and Dorian exchanged glances, unsure whether revealing their true natures would be advisable here in Faerie.

"Well, it has been wonderfully pleasant chatting with you youngsters," said Charles. "But I must be away now, as the sun is rising."

"You can't be out in the sunlight?"

"It's not so much a matter of *can't*," said Charles, "only that we fade away in the light, much like the mist we are made out of. I have tried a few experiments myself, including achieving solidity, but unfortunately unless the day is very grey and cold, we become insubstantial. As I can see the sun is breaking over the hills, I don't have much more time."

True to his words, Leah and Dorian could see the ghost convocation packing up and some of the ghosts already drifting away.

"But you will come back and visit soon?" asked Charles hopefully. "I do so like to hear the news."

"If we can," said Dorian.

"It's been a pleasure to speak with you," said Charles, and he floated away towards the other ghosts.

The sun broke, bright and orange and pink in the sky.

Moments afterward, Dorian and Leah were alone on the hilltop.

CHAPTER SEVEN

The two detectives sat together on the side of the hill and watched the sun rise.

Nothing seemed particularly pressing. Neither spoke. Just two best friends witnessing dawn breaking over the world.

***

Once day had well and truly arrived, they began making their way back across the Fae mirror-city of Glasgow. They stopped in front of the bakery to press their noses against the warm golden-lit glass. They threw skipping stones across the Clyde. They played in every playground they passed. By the time they had reached Beira's flat, it was nearly noon.

Nobody had bothered them. One of the bakers had even offered them a treat. But Dorian and Leah, being who they were, knew not to accept an offer of food in Faerie.

Not in these parts, anyway.

Beira's house was another story entirely.

"There you are!" exclaimed Beira, who was standing in the doorway, waiting for them. "I trust you had a good day out? Lunch is waiting."

Leah and Dorian made their way inside, and they cheerfully shouted over each other as they took the ham and cheese toasties on offer and ate them, getting crumbs all over the floor.

"And all good things come to an end, as all good things must," said Beira. "Sit on the sofa, children, and I will bring you some tea and biscuits."

Leah and Dorian climbed up onto the couch. Dorian had a bit of string in his pocket, so they played cat's cradle until Beira returned with the tea.

"Drink up," she said. "I've given you an extra chocolate biscuit each."

"Thank you!" they chorused, and then practiced the ancient ritual of dunking the biscuit into the tea just long enough to get it soggy but *not* long enough so it crumbled into the tea. It was an art form.

The night must have been a long one, because Leah felt very drowsy. The sofa was so comfortable, too. She put her tea down on the side-table carefully because she was having a hard time keeping her eyes open.

Leah leaned back against the couch, and within minutes, fell fast asleep.

"You know what they say," said Beira, as Leah dreamily opened her eyes again for a brief moment, "You cannae throw your granny aff the bus, and you also can't tell her there are things you haven't forgotten. Things only children and the old folks know. What matters, what *really* matters, when it all falls away? Fun, adventure, memories – but most of all, fast friends."

Dorian woke a while later, and Leah saw a look of relief followed by vague disappointment cross his face.

"It has been a long, long while since you were a child, my handsome seal-pup," said Beira. "I thought it would be a good experience for you to visit childhood again."

Beira handed Leah a bag of sour gummies.

"Here," she said. "It is this you've been chasing; you'll never find it in a bottle. There is no age in which you must stop having fun or stop enjoying candy in favour of alcohol. All these things have been forgotten by many. It's important that you remember."

Old Man Snorfles looked up at the bag hopefully. Leah tucked it into the pocket of her worn leather jacket.

"I don't think these are for you," she told him, but Beira handed her a dog biscuit, and she offered it to him. Old Man Snorfles held out a paw with a little whuff and some difficulty, and Leah shook it. "Delighted to make your acquaintance, Sir Snorfles."

"Oh, don't be callin' him that, he'll be giving himself airs," said Beira, but Snorfles seemed delighted, crunching down on the dog biscuit with loud gusto.

"Thank you, Beira," said Leah, with honest gratitude.

Dorian stood, adjusting his waistcoat, and nodded his agreement.

"Yes, thank you," said Dorian. "It was an experience I shall look back on fondly."

"But I take it you must be going," said Beira. They both nodded. "A detective never rests. Always working. That is just the way of the world, is it not? The work, the work is never done. I shall soon end my holidays here so I may return to the oceans and mountains to wash the plaid. But I have promised a warm autumn, and so you shall have one."

"I appreciate it," said Leah.

Beira handed them a little box of digestive biscuits and then followed them to the door. Old Man Snorfles did the same, wagging his tail a little.

"Goodbye," Beira said. "And when the first snow falls, think of me."

***

Leah and Dorian made their way back, through the city streets and market stalls. When they finally found their way into the waiting room, they surprised some kind of creature that had been reading a newspaper. It fled, no doubt to sound whatever alarm they had in this part of Faerie.

But that was all right, because they were leaving.

They went through the wall and climbed the stairs. Dorian tapped at the roof of the staircase with his walking stick.

There was no answer.

He tapped a bit louder.

Suddenly, a hatch opened above them, pouring light into the darkness.

It was Aoife. She beckoned them up and out of the stairwell, a finger pressed to her lips.

They crawled out and into the bedroom, where they saw that Caoimhe was fast asleep on the floor, blond hair tumbling around her pink cheeks.

Leah knelt down and put the bag of sour gummies and little box of cookies beside her.

"For an excellent sentinel," she whispered.

***

Aoife said her farewells at the door, explaining that she needed to look after Caoimhe when she awoke.

Leah and Dorian made their way back to Interpol.

As they stood beside the red-sandstone castle coffeeshop that served as the marker for the police station, Leah paused.

"Something the matter?" asked Dorian.

Leah gave him a half-grin.

"You know what?" she said. "No."

She pressed her palm flat to the stone, and a brief glow surrounded it. A door opened in the wall, and Leah went inside, with Dorian following a moment afterward.

They descended the stairs surrounded by mysterious vegetation and even more enigmatic tiny lights that giggled and snickered from behind the leaves, casting a late-evening luminescence on the staircase and pathway that led to Caledonia Interpol. Sometimes the archways were full of flowers, sometimes they were not, but they were always green and beautiful.

Leah and Dorian went in the door and turned left, past the great arching window that looked out onto the mysterious fog and mist outdoors, through which the tree-branch arms of strange shadow-creatures were dimly visible, and then walked down the corridor to the Great Hall.

The weather had taken a turn for the worse. Fog rolled softly through the room and brought in a sort of chill that dissipated as it was chased away by the massive fire roaring in the enormous fireplace. The brass firedogs played and bounded back and forth in the firelight and shadow.

❀ CHAPTER SEVEN ❀

Leah and Dorian took their usual places on the sofa in front of the fire. Their laptops bounced over on their little antique-brass legs. Leah patted hers on the back of the screen as the computers both jumped up on the sofa and settled beside them like dogs.

The pixies had just delivered afternoon tea complete with little cakes and sandwiches on a cart when Chief Ben rumbled past.

"You two have desks, you know," he grumbled. "Dorian, you have a visitor."

Dorian shot Leah a puzzled look. They turned to see a very handsome man with large, mournful, whisky-coloured eyes standing in the doorway.

"Hello, Robert," said Dorian. Leah nodded a greeting.

"Leah, will you please excuse me?"

"Of course," said Leah, and she watched Dorian get up and go to the entryway to greet the vampire poet of Scotland.

Then she turned away to give them some privacy.

Leah took a sip of her tea, contemplating the fire.

CHAPTER EIGHT

eah did not have to wait long, because Dorian returned within a half hour.

She was startled to see something like tears brimming in his eyes.

"Can we –" Dorian began. He swallowed. "Can we talk?"

Everything that had been sour between them seemed to melt away.

"Yes, of course," said Leah, full of sudden concern.

"Elsewhere," said Dorian. "Not so public."

"Okay," Leah replied. "The labyrinth?"

Dorian nodded his agreement.

"What do you need?" she asked quietly.

She had never seen such emotion in his expression.

Then he met her eyes.

"I need my best friend."

***

Leah stood with Dorian in the entrance to the labyrinth. She often got lost there, but the Minotaur had a soft spot for her and always returned her to the office. This was also the only way to access the laboratory, where Dr. Milo McFintan, *ceasg* scientist, did the autopsies and some questionable experiments. He was joined by Hazel Bloodworth, sixties fashion icon and ghost, the former wife of one of Glasgow's greatest criminals, Sebastian.

"I hope Milo doesn't mind us hanging out here," said Leah. "He likes an air of mystery around his work. Makes him creepier, he says."

"I'm sure it's fine," said Dorian.

"So, what happened?" asked Leah.

Dorian sighed.

"Robert wishes to end this – this – whatever it is we have together," said Dorian on a shaky note. "He says his only thoughts will always be of Desdemona, and he feels it is unfair to me since he is now, always has been, and believes he always will be, consumed by her."

"He wishes he were consumed by her," Leah remarked in a snide tone. "I'm sorry to hear that, Dorian. I really thought something might come of it."

"I, too," said Dorian, and now tears tracked down his cheeks. "And I was resistant, at first, but he talked me into it."

"Well, you know I've always thought he was an arsehole," said Leah.

"I thought you had dreams about him."

Leah rolled her eyes, caught.

"Well, yeah," she allowed. "I mean, he's – well, look at him. Anyway. Who cares? Doesn't make him less of an arsehole. But look –"

She sighed and ran a hand through her hair. Then she leaned back against the wall and crossed her arms.

"This experience taught you – has taught *us,* that the Fae don't necessarily *have* to be bound to their stories," she said. "We've seen it again and again. Now it doesn't seem so much fact as a tenet of faith. We had our suspicions before, but isn't this proof? And if it happened once, Dorian, it could happen again. If Robert chooses to return to the safe confines of *his* story, then that's his choice. But don't you see? Now we know it's a *choice.* Maybe there is someone else in the future for you."

Dorian considered her words, and then nodded.

"Foolish, isn't it, weeping over a man so many have wept over," he said. "I should have known. His loyalty to anyone but Desdemona was never exactly famed."

"It's not foolish," said Leah. "It's normal. It's –"

She grinned.

"Human."

They stood there and stared at each other for a while, wondering what this revelation might mean. Not only for them, but the entire Fae world.

"It's not so bad, being human," said Leah. "I've been one all my life."

"It's not that, believe me," said Dorian. "I'm a selkie; as such, have always admired humanity. It's only that I've always lived this one way, and centuries have passed since I knew another life. I don't know what these changes mean, and I do not wish to hide from you that I find such change somewhat frightening."

"Again, sounds pretty human to me," said Leah, and took his hand. "Dorian, listen. I know I kept you at arm's length because of everything – before. But maybe there are other relationships just as important as romantic love. And, well. I'm ready to listen now."

Dorian gave her a look filled with such hope and gratitude that her heart ached.

"Truly?"

"Truly."

Dorian looked her in the eye.

"Leah, I cannot express how sorry I am," he confessed. "There are no words for what you mean to me. Losing Robert is difficult, but in a long life such as mine, such losses would have been negligible, had I not been a Taken selkie. Because I hadn't experienced romantic loss in centuries, this was quite the blow, and I think Robert was aware of that, given how softly he tread. But nothing in my eternal life has ever hit so hard as the idea that I might lose your friendship."

"Same here," admitted Leah. "I may not be eternal, and I may not be Fae, but... I've missed you."

Dorian favoured her with one of his slight smiles.

"Still," he insisted, "I cannot pretend the mistakes of the past are not my mistakes to own. When I saw what my brother had done to Dahlia – or, at least, if it *wasn't* Magnus that committed the act, he certainly buried the body – and I kept silent...that was a great sin on my part, and I cannot help but wonder if it led directly to the actions that brought you into my orbit for the first time. I do not know, indeed, whether Magnus has committed other atrocities without my knowledge. That is guilt I will have to live with forever, and since the Fae cannot die unless killed, that may be a good long time to come."

He paused for a moment, deep in thought.

"All I can do is apologise," he said. "I understand it is little consolation, and inadequate, but it is all I have to offer. And from this day forward, I give you my solemn vow to always be as transparent and truthful as possible. I know my actions hurt you, and I have no right to expect your bosom companionship anymore. But know this, Leah – until you, I had been alone. I thought I should always be alone. That is the lot of the Taken selk, those who are left behind. Then, there was you. And I was not alone anymore. That is worth all the gold in this world and the next."

Now Leah could feel tears slipping down her own cheeks.

"Damn it," she said, wiping them away angrily.

She sighed.

"Me too," she said again. And then, after a pause:

"I don't know if I forgive you."

Dorian looked crestfallen.

"I don't know if I *should* forgive you," she clarified. "But you're the best thing that ever happened to me, you and – and all this."

She waved, indicating Interpol, the labyrinth, and the Fae world in general.

"When Beira turned us into kids, I don't know," said Leah. "Everything that seemed so important and worthwhile just sort of...faded away. None of that stuff mattered. Well, obviously it *mattered*, but it just didn't seem like such a big deal. Hanging out with friends, doing cool stuff, all that seemed a lot more important, and the thing is – I'm just another drunk in an old leather jacket, another stereotype. What am I even worth? I sure didn't think I'd end up like – *this* – as a kid. But you, when I met you, with you –"

Leah wiped the tears away again.

"You made me feel like I was worth something," she said. "Like my knowledge mattered, like folklore mattered, who *I am* mattered. Caledonia in general, of course; getting recruited to the Fae police was not something I'd expected to put on my CV. But you, Dorian Grey – I mattered to *you*."

They leaned together, then pressed their foreheads together. Leah, on impulse, hugged him.

"So," said Dorian. "Maybe not forgiven, not entirely, but –"

"Starting over."

Dorian nodded his head against hers, and he returned the hug.

"Starting over."

***

Once they had made themselves presentable again, they returned to the Interpol office.

Chief Ben looked up from his desk and eyed them warily.

"This better not be some kind of office romance," he said.

Leah nearly jumped out of her skin.

"Wow, no," she declared, then looked at Dorian. "Er. Sorry. No offence."

Dorian inclined his head.

"None taken, Miss Bishop."

He looked askance at their boss.

"Are they forbidden, office romances?" he asked. "Out of interest."

"No, they're just stupid," said Chief Ben. "Glad to see you're patching things up, though. Here's the latest on your case."

He slid a sheet of paper across the desk. They leaned forward to read it.

Dorian was the first to straighten up. There was a question on his face all the way up to his eyebrows.

"Time travel?" Leah said aloud, asking the question on Dorian's face. "And just how are we supposed to do that?"

"Beats me," grumbled Chief Ben, taking a drink of his industrial-strength coffee in his industrial-sized mug. "I just work here."

CHAPTER NINE

h, hell. What do you want?"

"We're here on police business, Aonghas," said Dorian.

"Don't flip that badge at me, I already know who you are."

Aonghas was sitting on the fountain in Kelvingrove Park, because it was a lovely day and that was what all Glaswegians did when the sun was out.

He was slender, and ethereally beautiful, even though he had a rough, lived-in look. Aonghas was a Trooping Faerie, and as Glasgow changed, so did he. Centuries ago, he wore long green raiment, and his magic satchel was filled with wine and bread. Today, he had a shamrock tattoo on his neck and wore the Celtic colours. His magic satchel invariably offered him curry and Buckfast.

His apprentice, Dylan, was approaching them, white wings spread wide and feathers trailing in the sunshine. Dylan was dressed in Rangers blue, but that was authentic, because he had only recently come into his Fae inheritance. Dylan was something of a bruiser, stocky and strong.

"Leah, Dorian," Dylan greeted them.

"Dylan," Dorian nodded.

"We need you to send us back in time," said Leah.

"And why would I do that?" asked Aonghas.

"Because you don't want to spend the rest of eternity in the Deeps?"

Aonghas sniffed.

"You can't do that," he declared. "It's illegal."

Leah sighed.

"Then as a favour for a friend?"

Aonghas gave her a long look, then nodded.

"Should've opened with that, really," he said. "Just how big a favour?"

"We're trying to get to the time when the vampire with iron

teeth was first seen in the Necropolis," explained Leah.

Aonghas rubbed his hands.

"Hm. Medium sized. Okay. Are you ready?"

"You haven't been at the pub recently, have you?" asked Dorian with faint concern.

"I know how to do my job," said Aonghas archly. "So, you want to do this or not?"

"Sorry, Aonghas," said Leah. "Don't listen to him. Yes, please."

Dorian gave her a *look* and she held back a laugh.

"Okay," said Aonghas. "You have to concentrate on the time period you want to be in, think *hard* on it. Do you know when it is you'd like to be? Exact dates and places, I mean."

"Yes," chorused Dorian and Leah.

"Okay," said Aonghas. "Then keep both in mind, concentrate, and be ready."

Dylan was calmly eating curry out of a polystyrene box, sitting on the fountain, as Aonghas lifted his hands, and they began to crackle with a white, electric light.

"Good luck," said Aonghas. "Time wants to go back to normal, so don't tarry. Understood? You get lost in the time stream, I might not be able to get you back. If, that is, I bother to go looking."

"Understood," said Dorian, and Leah nodded.

Aonghas turned his palms outward, and the light shot out from them. There was a loud *pop*, and Leah could've sworn she heard Dylan yell, but it was indistinct.

Then, suddenly, all was quiet, and the sun was gone.

***

Glasgow in the past was not the city it had become by Leah's time.

The weather was cold and damp, unwelcoming with a chill and bitter wind. Poverty reigned and the terror of hunger stalked the streets, gripping with skeletal hands.

Leah and Dorian stood beneath towering tenement blocks

that had fallen into disrepair. Entire walls were missing, as if they had been bombed out – and some certainly were. Glasgow had suffered during the Blitz. But these buildings had fallen into disrepair for other reasons more mundane. Neglect and poverty.

The holes in the buildings exposed the families within to the elements, but they had no other choice. A roof over their heads was a roof, at least. Curtains fluttered through the openings, in a vain attempt to keep in something like warmth.

It was nighttime, and they could hear a woman singing to her child. Leah could see her through the wide hole in the wall, holding her baby to her chest.

"This is –"

"The early 70s," Leah said. "Not the 50s. Why are we here?"

"Aonghas's magic is volatile," said Dorian. "Sometimes we also find that what we need is more important than what we want. Often, that is what guides it."

"Like Beira's magic," said Leah.

"Yes."

The horrors of Glasgow tenement life were difficult for Leah to witness. She knew about them, of course; they were a part of the historical study of Scotland at university, but she had forgotten how recent that life had been, and how many children had grown up in this kind of abject poverty in the city she called home.

"I suppose we will be able to ask adults about the vampire," said Dorian. "They may have seen it as children. Although that plan of action hardly seems promising."

"Or," said Leah, on a hunch, "it happened here, too, but who was going to listen to anybody in this derelict, forgotten place?"

Her love for the city was even stronger now, and the heartache at seeing what people had to suffer through went deep into her bones like the damp Glaswegian weather.

Then, she began to recognise the song the woman was singing to her child in the tenement window, and after a moment, to recite it along with her.

"Whatna noise is that I hear
Comin' doon the street?
Weel I ken the dump-dump
O' her beetle feet.
Mercy me, she's at the door,
Hear her lift the sneck;
Whisht! An' cuddle mammy noo
Closer roun' the neck.

Jenny wi' the airn teeth,
The bairn has aff his claes,
Sleepin' safe an' soun', I think –
Dinna touch his taes;
Sleepin' weans are no for you;
Ye may turn about
An' tak' awa' wee Tam next door—
I hear him screichin' oot."

"A fine song to sing to a child," said Dorian, his words laced with a tinge of horror.

"Terror is an important aspect of childlore," said Leah. "Dorian, what if Jenny wi' the airn teeth was manifested by the children after their parents sang this song to them?"

"It's possible," said Dorian. "But why only at these specific intervals in time? Shouldn't she be something of a permanent fixture?"

Leah looked around at the broken windows, the rubbish everywhere, the crumbling walls.

"There's not much call for monsters in a place that has no hope," added Dorian.

"Or a monster is a welcome distraction," said Leah. "For the children, they may not even be aware their situation is a dire one. Remember how we felt? Things adults cared about didn't matter anymore. A monster, though – especially a monster they could *fight*, and maybe they could be heroes –"

"That might give them hope indeed."

CHAPTER TEN

"hat song's wrong, ye ken," said a voice somewhere in the vicinity of their knees.

Dorian and Leah looked down to see a child around ten years of age. He looked up at them with a pair of large dark eyes beneath a thatch of brown hair. He was dirty and his knees were skinned, evident beneath the baggy shorts that hung off his emaciated frame. He also wore an inexplicably immaculate t-shirt. Exposure to the elements didn't seem to bother him despite the wintry weather. One of his socks had fallen down, sagging around the ankle.

"You polis?" asked the kid. Leah nodded. "Huh. Didn't think the polis ever came round here."

"Well, we are here today," said Dorian. "What do you mean, the song's wrong?"

"Awfu' posh accent you got for weegie polis," remarked the kid. He wiped his nose on his sleeve. "Anybody knows, it's a *vampire* wi' airn teeth. No' Jenny. The monster 'round here, I mean. Everybody kens it."

"Vampire with iron teeth?" Leah repeated back. The kid nodded. "And you say it's around here?"

"Aye."

"Can you show us?" she asked.

The kid mulled it over, then nodded and set out across the wide, empty lot littered with rubbish and broken bricks.

They followed him through the decay and rubble of the tenement housing, all the way out to the hill beyond the Gorbals settlements.

"You can see it from over there," he said, pointing. "In the Necropolis."

"The –"

Leah and Dorian exchanged looks.

"No' as fancy as the big one, but does the job fine," said the kid with pride.

"No *wonder* the ghosts didn't know what we were talking about," Leah told Dorian under her breath, and he nodded his agreement. "This is the *Southern Necropolis,* not the Necropolis!"

"Have you seen it?" asked Dorian, turning his attention back to the boy. "The vampire?"

"Everybody's *seen* it," said the kid. "I'm just no' superstitious like the rest o' the weans."

"You are very grown-up," Leah assured him. The kid nodded, as if this were a given.

"We're new here," said Dorian. "Could you point it out to us?"

"Sure," said the kid with a shrug, and they followed him into the graveyard.

***

It was smaller than the city's Necropolis, but as the kid had said, it got the job done.

The Southern Necropolis was a flat green rectangle of a field beyond the tenements. Many of the graves were in disrepair, covered with bright-green ivy. Large trees stood over some of the stones, giving the place a sombre atmosphere.

"There it is," said the kid, pointing. "Vampire wi' airn teeth, like I said."

Standing before them was nothing other than one of the great new buildings across the Clyde, all modernity and glass, the spires of its roof pointing toward the sky.

"September 23, 1954, hundreds of children ran into the Necropolis, armed with stakes," Leah said aloud, as if reciting from a book. "And generation after generation of children found their own vampires to hate and to hunt."

Forward progress always upset someone.

"Looks like it got teeth. Fangs, ye ken," said the boy, indicating the spires.

He regarded the building with some interest.

"But see, me…I like stories about the future," said the kid

after a time. "I don't see what's so great about holdin' on to – well."

He gestured towards the state of the tenement buildings.

"Thank you for your help," said Leah.

"Can I go now?" asked the kid.

"Yes," said Dorian.

"Thanks, pal," said the boy, and he scampered off.

"We should probably be going as well," said Leah. "Aonghas did warn us not to linger, after all."

"Agreed," said Dorian, and they followed in the wake of the kid, who had already disappeared somewhere into the maze of the tenements.

As they passed the woman singing to her child, this time, the song was different.

"Dorian," said Leah, "Wait."

Dorian paused and listened to the song that floated down from the broken tenement wall.

"...neither ken I my bairnie's faither
nor yet the land where he bides in.
I am a man upon the land
I am a selkie on the sea..."

Dorian smiled, despite himself.

"So," said Leah. "They *did* have hope, after all."

***

After Leah and Dorian returned to the office, she made her excuses, claiming she had a coffee date and would catch up with them later.

After assuring the chief she would bring him at least a pot of coffee from the shop, she was allowed to leave, with a promise she would return by the early morning.

As the sun set over Glasgow, Leah entered the coffeehouse that stood sentinel over the Interpol office, in the little castle-like building that served as the entrance to Caledonia.

Now, she sat at a table in the room upstairs, taking a sip of delicious coffee.

She sensed him before she saw him. When she looked up, her eyes snagged as if she could not look anywhere else, her gaze caught by the image of the man walking into the room.

But this had always been par for the course, for Robert Burns.

Robert was not only handsome. Any man could be that. He was much, much more. There was something of an inner fire to him that lit up his good looks as if he were incandescent.

He had long caught the eye of everyone who had known him. As a man, he had already been notable and distinguished for a multitude of reasons, from his striking features to his talent with poetry.

As a vampire, all of this was now intensified – except his writing, which he had found himself unable to do ever since the change.

Until now.

The light picked up the whisky-glow of his amber eyes, sweet as honey. They were illuminated from within, a strange quirk of his features which had even predated his supernatural turn and had been written about by no less a man than Sir Walter Scott. This trait had stayed with him when he had crossed over from human to vampire. He had been impossibly sired by the *baobhan sith* who held his unwanted heart in her taloned hands. Beyond all expectation, just by sheer faith in his love for her, in his unwavering belief that she *could*.

In this way, he'd already witnessed a change of story.

Cad or not, Robert Burns believed in love.

Today, he wore a loose white shirt with the top buttons open and tight black trousers.

He *also* did this because he was Robert Burns.

He sat down across from Leah.

She kicked him hard under the table.

"Ow!" yelped Robert. "Leah!"

"That was for Dorian," said Leah, taking a nonchalant sip of her coffee.

"That's why you asked me to meet you?" said Robert, rubbing his shin. "So you could kick me?"

"Be grateful I didn't give you a Glasgow kiss," said Leah. "How could you do that to him?"

Robert sighed.

"I didn't like to," he admitted. "The water under the bridge, well. It's quite sour at this point."

"You *do* know that you don't need to *live inside the boundaries of your story* anymore," said Leah. "You're not cursed, Robert."

Robert smiled warmly. She hated how obnoxiously handsome he was, and how his soothing voice sounded like water over pebbles in a clear, bright stream.

Bastard.

"I know," said Robert. "And I thank both you and Dorian for discovering it. But you must know I never thought myself cursed. Not the way Dorian always did. We are all different, Leah."

"And you'd rather be in unrequited love with a monster that does not even have the capacity to love you back?" asked Leah, hating how her words seemed to echo Sebastian's. That confrontation seemed so long ago.

"Robert, you can make a *choice* now –"

"But don't you see?" he told her. "I have made my choice. And this is what I chose. It doesn't matter if Des can or can't love me back, Leah. It's never mattered to me, as I've told you before. But how much more a grand gesture of love is it, if it's *not* a curse, but a choice? A curse means you're forced. A choice means – well, that you choose, and every day of my existence, I have come to understand, I will always, and forever, choose her."

Robert slid a hand through his black hair, pulling it back into a ponytail.

Damn, thought Leah. **Everything** *this guy does is sexy.*

"And so I thought it was unfair to Dorian. As I've told you

105

both before, many times, Jeannie deserved better. The others, too. So I tried, Leah. I really did – but this time, I didn't want to be selfish. This time, I thought I'd make the right choice. So I didn't want to do the same thing to Dorian. I thought you'd agree he deserves better, too."

Leah didn't have much to say to that, because of course she was in total agreement with the sentiment, especially when it came to Dorian.

"Excuse me for a moment," said Robert. "I'd like to get some coffee myself."

Leah sat and thought about what Robert had said, as she waited for him to return. She hated to admit it, but it made sense. If the Fae could choose, then what right did she have to insist he did or did not do anything? That was the point of choice.

Robert returned with a fancy whipped drink that smelled like –

"Is that a pumpkin spice latte?" Leah demanded.

"Some kind of special they had," he said. "Flavours are all strange to me, since I have a...very *particular* kind of diet, but I can't help but find all these advancements impressive. We didn't have these things in my day."

Leah wished Robert's smile wasn't so disarming. She wished the things he said didn't seem so reasonable, didn't seem to make perfect sense. He made people want to care for him, and that was a dangerous kind of man.

"So what's your plan?" she asked. "Are you going back to your pub in the Highlands, to guard the door to Faerie again? Or staying in the city, to keep haunting Desdemona?"

"Now that I've decided," said Robert, "and made a choice – I don't know. I think I will go back, at least to ensure that things are in order. I've been away for a spell, and I hope it hasn't been to the detriment of either the pub, or to Faerie. By the by, I hear you live there now."

"Yes," Leah agreed. "And I was just there with Dorian, in the underworld."

Robert gave her a stern look.

"I don't think that was altogether safe," he said. "Why didn't you ask me, or Desdemona, or even Nour for help?"

"Because sometimes we have to do our jobs on our own, Robert. Vampires can't help us all the time."

Robert sighed and stirred his pumpkin spice latte.

"Noted," he said.

She narrowed her eyes.

"Although you may be of help with this one. You haven't heard of a vampire with iron teeth, have you?" she asked.

"That the latest thing?" he replied. "Last I heard about something like that, it was the fifties or thereabouts."

"The stories seem to crop up again from time to time. Seems we are in the reappearance part of that cycle."

"No, sorry," he said. "I've never heard of anything like that, apart from the old stories about the kids in the cemetery. But I'm no expert when it comes to these things. That would be Desdemona's remit."

He paused.

"So, do you want to kick me in the leg again, or catch up on our lives?"

"Oh, just one more time for the hell of it," she said.

"Ow!"

"Okay, *now* we can catch up."

CHAPTER ELEVEN

The morning had come, swift and sure, after Leah had spent most of the night talking to Robert in the coffeeshop. Ben received his pot of coffee, so not a word was said about her absence from the filing of paperwork.

"Dorian," said Leah. "Come and look at this."

Dorian walked across the office to where Leah was seated near one of the immense bookcases that took up an entire wall of Interpol, reading up on folklore.

He didn't speak for a moment. She noted the raincloud expression on his face.

"Is this about me talking to Robert?" she asked.

"The last thing that man needs is further reason for arrogance."

"I kicked him in the shin," she said, turning back to the book in her hand and paging through it. "Twice."

"Indeed?" asked Dorian, a little hopeful lilt to his voice.

Leah looked up at him and burst out laughing.

"Yeah," she said. "And I'll do it again for good measure if you want. Anything for my best friend. But –"

Dorian sat down in a wingback chair with a sigh.

"But?"

"Listen," she said. "Robert pointed out that the important thing we've learned here, is *choice*."

"So he *chooses* unrequited love?" asked Dorian, faintly surprised. "Why?"

Leah shrugged.

"Who the hell knows?" she said. "He thinks it's a bigger sacrifice or some shit. He's Robert Burns. There's not much that can explain DJ Rabbie B."

"Is this some new nickname I was unaware of?"

"Guess so."

Dorian shook his head at himself.

"A selkie's inclination is toward the romantic," he said. "I suppose it was foolish of me to expect, well, much of anything from him."

"It wasn't foolish," said Leah. "But he said this was his choice, and if we want to talk about *choice* as the important thing here, we have to respect it, no matter how stupid it seems to us. And I suppose it *is* romantic, in its own way."

"Very well," said Dorian. "I understand. And I thank you for your service."

Leah laughed again.

"Anytime, Dorian Grey."

"Now, what is it you wanted to show me?"

"Oh," said Leah, the book in her hands almost forgotten. "It was this discussion of folklore and illness. You know how they used to think porphyria was vampirism, autistic children were changelings, that kind of thing?"

"Yes," said Dorian. "Explanations for things they didn't have an explanation for. As Charles said in the Necropolis. People have an innovative way of interpreting things they don't understand."

"And that kid in the Gorbals," said Leah. "He said the new office building was referred to as a *vampire with iron teeth*. Something to do with progress, and also the fact that these beautiful buildings were going up across the Clyde when the people of the Gorbals were living in such poverty."

"That child," said Dorian slowly. "Did you not think he bore a resemblance to someone we know?"

Leah thought about it.

"Dylan," she said.

***

But Aonghas did not have good news for them.

"I don't like to say it," he told them, "but when you vanished, he vanished too."

"You sent *him* back in time?!" exclaimed Leah. "Nice aim, pal."

Aonghas shot her a dirty look.

"Next time, you can do your own time-travel, Detective," he said loftily.

Leah shut her mouth.

"Sorry," she said. "That was uncalled for. But would that have been Dylan back there, in that time period? The little boy in the Gorbals?"

"It might have been," Aonghas said. "But if that's where he had ended up from the accidental time-travel, he'd have been a grown man, not a child like you saw. Although it is possible his presence here translated to bringing you to see him during his childhood there. There's real power in that. Dylan is the Guardian of Glasgow Green for a reason. He grew up in the Gorbals."

"So that may have been his mother as well," said Dorian, "who we heard singing."

"There's only one person who can confirm that, and he's missing," said Leah. "Great. Have you tried calling him?"

Aonghas gave her a strange look.

"What do you think I've been doing since you left?" he asked. "I've looked everywhere and haven't found him yet. I've tried everything."

The concern in Aonghas's voice belied the faerie's usual blasé demeanour. Dylan was Aonghas's student, and it was clear he was far more worried than he let on.

"Well, didn't you say we had to concentrate on the time period we wished to visit?" asked Dorian. "If he was hit by the spell, then it would pull him to wherever, or whenever, he had on his mind."

"What time period would Dylan have had on his mind?" asked Leah.

"Oh," said Aonghas. He stood up quickly from the fountain. "Oh, shit."

"I take it this is not a positive development," said Dorian.

"No, it's not," said Aonghas. "It's – he'd have gone back in time to see Tearlach, but –"

"But?"

"I sensed angel-magic, too," said Aonghas. "Hanging around here like someone sprayed it in the air. The perfume is undeniable. Angels tend to leave a mark."

"What does that mean?"

"They're messy. I wouldn't recommend one as a pet."

"No, I meant what does that mean for Dylan?"

"Oh. A parting gift from Nuriel, would be my guess," said Aonghas. "Which means he might be stuck back there."

"What, forever?" asked Leah. Aonghas nodded.

"Angels have funny ideas about what constitutes a gift."

Then he said:

"I can keep searching, at least now that I know where to look. But no guarantees."

"Okay," said Leah. "Let us know what happens, if anything."

"Good luck," said Aonghas.

"You too."

***

Leah and Dorian took the subway to Partick, where they found themselves walking the aisles of Morrison's aimlessly.

"I don't approve of most of the food in this store," sniffed Dorian.

"Well, we can go to Waitrose afterwards, you snob," said Leah. "The food probably disapproves of you, too."

"I'm not a snob just because I enjoy the finer things in life."

"That is literally what a snob is, Dorian Grey."

"What about Marks & Spencer?"

"How can I actually *hear* the ampersand in that sentence?"

"I didn't know you knew that word, Miss Bishop."

"*Snob.*"

"We can go to Majestic Wines afterwards if you like."

"Now you're talking."

"Leah," said Dorian, pulling her aside in the dairy aisle, where she was examining some options for Devonshire clotted cream. "There's – something –"

Leah looked up and nearly dropped the jar in her hand.

Darkness was filling the Morrison's, and it was clear this was not a power blackout.

A shadow fell as dark mist rolled across the cereal aisle.

"What the –" Leah managed to say, just before the darkness engulfed them both.

CHAPTER TWELVE

There was a chittering sound from a few aisles away.

"What the hell was that?"

"Shh."

The chittering sound came again, along with a whispering noise that reminded Leah of an insect walking.

A very, very large one.

"Do you think it's the vampire?" asked Leah. "In the past, it may have been a euphemism for progress, but –"

"That doesn't sound like any vampire I have ever known," Dorian whispered back.

"Maybe *that* was a euphemism too," said Leah. "We never did find out what the vampire was the first time."

The selkie's eyes went wide.

"*On her beetle feet,*" said Dorian. "Do you think –"

But Leah didn't get a chance to ask Dorian what he thought she thought, because a nightmare horror had just rounded the corner.

It saw them and screamed.

It was enormous, at least the height of the aisle, and in the shape of a giant cockroach with an elderly woman's head affixed to the front. Long blond hair hung down, stringy and patchy, and she looked at them with white-ball eyes.

She screamed again with a mouth full of sharp teeth, clicking the spider-like mouth pincers together.

Iron teeth.

Leah threw the clotted cream at her, which struck her directly in the centre of the forehead.

It screamed again, just as Dorian shouted, "Run!" and Leah threw herself down the aisle as they made a break for the door.

They made it just in time, slamming the glass doors shut behind them, and the monster thumped into the door, ricocheting off it and screaming in thwarted fury.

"What are we going to do now?" hissed Leah in the ensuing

silence.

"I don't know, lob more clotted cream at it?" snarked Dorian.

"Dorian!"

"My apologies."

"Your apologies, my ar –"

"Look!"

As Dorian and Leah held the door closed, the fog gradually lifted, little by little, right before their eyes.

The monster vanished.

Eventually, everything went back to normal as they watched, and the other patrons of the grocery store resumed their shopping as if nothing had happened.

Their strange experience had belonged to them alone.

"What," said Leah, "the absolute fuck."

Dorian gave her a look. Leah glared daggers at him.

"This never would have happened at Waitrose," he sniffed.

***

"What, exactly, do you expect to accomplish when fighting a monster that can move in and out of reality at will?" asked Dorian, hurrying to catch up with Leah.

"Fludge can do that, too," said Leah. "I'm going home to get him."

"We don't know this is the same creature the children saw! Besides, I thought we were going to Majestic."

"Some other time."

"Leah –"

"Who's the drunk around here, me or you? I said *later*. We've got more pressing concerns."

"Miss Bishop, I know you're keen to have Fludge on the payroll as some kind of, I don't know, K9 cop," said Dorian, and if Leah had been in any other kind of mood, she'd have laughed at the mincing way Dorian said *K9 cop*. "But I don't believe it is the correct course of action at this juncture –"

"Dorian Grey, I will personally punt you into next week," said

Leah, "Fludge is going to be useful. I swear. So. Are you in or out? On my side or not?"

Dorian sighed.

"In," he said. "I'm always on your side, Leah. You know that."

Leah gave him a quick, warm smile, and they made their way to one of Faerie's better neighbourhoods.

***

"I must admit, Leah," said Dorian, impressed, "I cannot find fault in your choice of accommodation."

Leah lived in a terraced house in Faerie, rented to her by the creature she had caught illegally selling trinkets some time before. His name was Waffles, and as it turned out, he did that a lot.

"Good morning, Waffles," Leah sang as she walked past him, where he was currently arguing with a builder.

Waffles was standing with his hands on his hips or thereabouts, since where they were was anybody's guess. He was a perfectly round circle with hair sticking out every which way, and enormous sad eyes.

"Good morning, Miss Bishop," Waffles called out, before turning his attention back to the builder. "We agreed that you would have the work finished by now, it's been weeks!"

The great, lumbering creature beside him stood there with one massive finger hooked daintily through a teacup and took a slow bite of chocolate pastry.

"These things take time, Waffles," it boomed ponderously.

"Time, time," sighed Waffles, exasperated. "Something it seems we all have too much and too little of, my friend."

"Excellent. That's very philosophical of you," said the builder.

"So you will be finished soon?"

"These things take –"

"Time. Yes, you said."

Dorian and Leah walked into her house, leaving Waffles to his discussion with the builder.

Leah's house was bright and cheery, with a large window overlooking the strange landscape outside.

"Have a seat," Leah invited, and Dorian sat down as a mug of tea floated over to him, a spoon slowly stirring it.

"I had forgotten some of the little conveniences of Faerie," said Dorian, as he took the mug. "Shall I speak to your landlord about the squorbles?"

"Maybe later," said Leah, making *tch tch tch* noises. "He seems a little preoccupied at the moment. Besides, I'm not sure how threatening he can be, slumlord or not, given he's the size of a Pomeranian and his name is *Waffles*. Oh, there you are!"

A hideous little creature came bounding down the staircase, leaping onto Leah's shoulder. It was almost entirely mouth, and its maw was filled with jagged, uneven teeth, row upon row like a shark. Its small, round body was entirely covered with purple-grey fur. It had huge eyes and a batlike nose, large claws like a bird of prey, and a long grey naked tail with a tuft of purple-grey fur at the end.

"Aww, did you miss me?" asked Leah in a baby voice, as Fludge chirped and hooted, nuzzling against her head.

"I often forget just how ugly he is," said Dorian. "That is one of the ugliest creatures I have ever seen."

Fludge looked at Dorian, then whirred and chirped at him too.

"You'll hurt his feelings," said Leah.

"He can't understand English."

"You'll hurt *my* feelings," Leah amended.

"Wouldn't want that," said Dorian. "The clotted-cream bandit might strike again."

"You know, it's a wonder nobody cut your tongue out after all these years," said Leah.

"It really is," agreed Dorian. "Now, with what do you think Fludge can help us?"

"I'm not exactly sure," said Leah, sitting down on the sofa and taking the mug of tea that had floated there to join her. "But I do know he can move between worlds. I just don't understand why we didn't see the monster in the underworld, or when we were children, or when we travelled in time, but on a shopping trip to Morrison's."

"I've seen stranger things in Morrison's."

"You're on a roll today," said Leah. "But seriously. I feel like there's something we're missing, something right in front of us."

Dorian sat and thought about this for a while. Fludge bounced from one of Leah's shoulders to the other, as they all sat together in her bright little house in the good neighbourhood of the Good People.

Suddenly, he leaned forward and looked directly at Leah.

Then he said:

"What do you know about the gloaming?"

CHAPTER THIRTEEN

"The time-between-times," said Leah automatically. "When the Fae and the human world touch. Everybody knows that, Dorian."

"Not everybody knows the reason it's known," Dorian replied. "A long time ago, before Interpol, before monsters started policing the actions of other monsters, they used the time-between-times to get out and wreak havoc on the human world. Sometimes, people would accidentally cross over. Women would suddenly turn up pregnant, that kind of thing."

"What is it with you people and sex?" Leah asked, rolling her eyes. She gave Fludge a carrot, which he snuffled at and then inhaled, crunching it between his huge teeth happily. "Some guy at the Cathouse gets somebody pregnant, he's a jerk. Some elf does it, he gets a song that thousands of people sing for years."

"Perhaps the Glasgow Reel is a bit too celebratory of those actions," said Dorian. "It was another time."

"Well, there's always some excuse, isn't there?" Leah retorted. "I was drunk, it was another time."

Dorian smiled and sipped his tea.

"I don't even *want* to know what you're smiling about," said Leah. "Anyway, back to the gloaming. You think there are monsters using the gloaming again for access to the human world?"

"Those who are allowed to live in both worlds permanently – selkies like me, for example – are often the object of some envy," said Dorian. "In the past, there were also many creatures who were allowed free rein to haunt the lonely passageways of the Highlands, killing and eating humans."

"Like the *baobhan sith*," said Leah. "Who's making these rules?"

"I couldn't even venture a guess. I'm not old enough to remember. But monsters given this type of permission were not confined to the Highlands. The cities had their monsters, too."

"As if cities needed more monsters," said Leah.

"The countryside is rife with the human monster," Dorian reminded her. "As Sherlock Holmes once observed, at least in the cities, *somebody* will hear you scream."

"Yeah, but will they do anything about it?" Leah demanded.

"We can do very little about the actions of the general public, Miss Bishop."

"Okay. Understood. Back on track. The gloaming was once a hell of a lot more dangerous than it is today. But this creature didn't manifest, as far as we know, until the 1950s. That was long after Interpol was founded, here and everywhere else around the world."

"Do you remember when I told you, on your very first day at Caledonia, that the first entrance to Interpol we used was the result of budget cuts?" asked Dorian.

"Yeah."

"Well..." he said. "There was a time when our cuts were severe, far worse than the ones we've experienced lately. The Gorbals and the tenements weren't the only places that experienced poverty. There were problems at the office in those days too. The defences for places like the Deeps suffered from power outages –"

"Wait," Leah interrupted. "Are you trying to tell me that this thing might have *come* from Caledonia?"

"From the Deeps, yes," said Dorian. "And much like any other era this *vampire with the iron teeth* has appeared, the monster – if indeed it was a monster at all – was likely to have been something different. Every single time."

"You know what this means, don't you?"

Dorian nodded, white as a sheet.

"Frankly, I wish I hadn't thought of it at all."

***

The Deeps of Caledonia Interpol were the high-security prison located beneath the streets of Glasgow. They were in the depths of the earth, below the Labyrinth where Milo did questionable experiments and performed autopsies of the dead.

Dorian, Leah knew, hadn't given much thought to the Deeps in the past.

Not until it had become personal.

Who is judge and jury here? she had often wondered. *Who decides these punishments? Who decided the punishments for monsters locked up so long ago we've forgotten their names?*

But there was one prisoner here whose name and story would not be forgotten in a hurry.

In the low light beyond the door, Leah could see the vague shape of a man in the shadows. He walked forward into the soft glow cast from the bare bulbs of the prison hallway.

As always, he took her breath away.

If there was anyone who looked the part of a Fae lover, comely to the point of aching, it was this man.

His long, beautiful brown curls hung over his shoulder; his blonde highlights picked out by the light. His wide, soulful brown eyes were soft and loving, but there was nothing behind them. He had a face like perfect faultless porcelain, with dark shadows around his eyes that made them seem like they were rimmed with kohl. His elegant neck dimpled at the collarbone, and his body was lithe and fit beneath the clothing he wore.

He smiled, exposing straight white teeth behind full, plush coral lips.

"Hello, brother," said Magnus Grey.

***

"We've come to ask you a few questions," said Leah, stepping in front of Dorian.

Magnus turned the full force of his charm on her.

"Why, Miss Bishop," said Magnus, a strange note of yearning in his voice. "It's been so long. You look beautiful."

The worst part about it all was that Magnus never *seemed* like he was lying, or evil. He always sounded perfectly sincere.

That was the thing about sociopaths. They never rang those

alarm bells. And most people trusted their own judgement when someone like Magnus walked into their lives. On lower levels, there were plenty of people who couldn't believe when someone they knew and liked had done something horrible. Magnus was the same thing, just on a far larger scale.

"Have you noticed anything strange lately?" asked Leah.

"Strange like?" asked Magnus. His eyes flitted to his brother, who was studying the ceiling.

"Strange like monsters," said Leah.

Magnus laughed. It was light and airy, like windchimes, or a summer picnic.

It chilled Leah's blood, because she knew better than to believe it. But oh, how easy must it have been to believe?

"Leah," said Magnus with a flirtatious grin. "We're all monsters."

"Yes, but," she said, already starting to lose her patience with him a little, "the other –"

"What's that?" asked Magnus with a start.

"What's what?"

"That," he said, and she was surprised to hear something akin to terror in his voice. "Leah. I don't know how to tell you this, but there's – there's something on your shoulder."

Leah looked at Fludge, who had just jumped onto her shoulder in search of carrots. He bared his teeth at Magnus, staring at him as a little low growl rose in the back of his throat.

"Oh, this is – never mind what it is!" snapped Leah. "I asked you a question."

"I asked *you* a question."

"It's my pet, okay?" she said. "Now will you answer –"

"You have one of *those*," said Magnus, the silvery tone of his words dropped now in favour of dread, "as a *pet*."

"You know what it is? The species, I mean?"

"You don't?"

"Nobody seems to. I found it under my bed."

Magnus sighed.

"Save us from the dangerous actions of fools," he muttered.

Leah glared at him, and he took pity on her.

"That," he said, "is one of the deadliest monsters ever to exist."

Leah glanced at Fludge.

"What do you mean?"

"That scar," said Magnus, "across your pretty face, the one you got as a child?"

Leah traced the scar with her fingertips.

"It wasn't from this," she said. "It was a different kind of monster."

"Yes," said Magnus. "The monster that scratched you? It was an accident. It was trying to protect you from *that*."

Fludge whirred and rubbed her head, looking for more carrots.

"Fine, thanks for the info," she said. "I'd like to know how the hell you even know that, but we're here on business. Let's get back on topic, shall we?"

"Leah, it's *child lore*," insisted Magnus, ignoring her attempt to redirect the conversation. "Despite my other actions, I was a detective as well. You want some answers. Well, the ones you get may not be the ones you came to find. One of the problems with investigation and finding out the truth. And I'm telling you, that creature is – well. It was created from the nightmares of children."

Fludge was gnawing at Leah's lapel now since no carrots had yet appeared.

"C'mon, knock it off," said Leah, and Fludge let go of her collar.

"Still," said Magnus. "Fascinating. It does seem to behave like a pet."

"You want to tell us what it is, and why you know when nobody else at Interpol does?"

"Funny thing about prison," said Magnus. "You learn a lot. Maybe not the kinds of things criminals ought to be learning, but when you put us in with other criminals –"

"Point taken," said Leah. "Now out with it."

"The Spanish-speaking world calls it *El Cucuy, or El Coco*," said Magnus. "Consider that a freebie. Because I like you, Leah."

Leah balked. She looked at Fludge again with new eyes.

"I see the folklorist recognises the name. Having second thoughts?"

"If you're right, he may be just a puppy."

"And what will you do when he's all grown up?"

"Forget the pet for a moment," said Leah, all business again as she tried to regain control of the conversation. "We're investigating some alleged attacks that happened at the Southern Necropolis."

Magnus moved forward, his beautiful face framed by the window.

"Vampire with the iron teeth again?" he asked. Leah nodded. "Well, I can't say I've noticed anyone here escaping, but then someone *noticing* would go against the grain of a successful prison break, I'd imagine. I wouldn't necessarily see them if they didn't want to get caught. Even so, why wouldn't they escape through the Labyrinth, or terrorise Interpol itself?"

"Because," said Dorian, finally stepping forward. "Folklore doesn't run on logic, Magnus."

"Oh, so now you speak," said Magnus. "Awfully astute observation there, brother. Very philosophical. When did you figure that out, during all those years you wasted in whorehouses and opium dens? I hear opium works wonders for the philosophical mind."

Dorian bowed his head in shame.

"Let's try to do this without fighting," Leah interjected, and Magnus turned his attention back to her.

"My guess is that you'll have to go back there," said Magnus. "Back to when it began, find out the inciting incident."

"We've gone back in time," Dorian put in, regardless of Leah's attempts to get between the two of them. "We lost Dylan in the process."

"What? How did you manage to –" Magnus sighed. "Never mind. No, I meant *Leah* and Leah alone. Back to the 1950s when this all started. That was the first time we had a security breach, right? The first time since we both started working at Caledonia, anyhow."

"And the second time was in the seventies," said Dorian.

"Budget cuts," agreed Magnus.

"Just like now," said Leah.

"Why can't I accompany Miss Bishop?" asked Dorian.

"For a seal who time-travels a lot, you certainly don't seem to remember the rules," said Magnus in a tetchy voice. "Interpol works for all Interpol employees regardless of the era, or we wouldn't use time-travel as often as we do. By this point, Aonghas should be issuing carnets. But it's because you can't meet yourself. You know that, Dorian."

"Then –"

"She'll have to find some way to convince you, and Ben, back in those days, that she's on the up and up," said Magnus.

"And you. She'll have to convince you, too."

Magnus smiled.

"That's right," he said. "I'll be there. But Leah."

Leah forced herself to look at him again. It was difficult to do it for very long, and too easy to be swayed by his spell.

"You *cannot* let on that you know – well," said Magnus. "Anything about me at all. You can't change history."

"We'll see about that," said Leah. Magnus's serene expression didn't change. "And that doesn't worry you?"

"The thing about trying to change history," said Magnus, "is that it never turns out quite as you'd expected. And if I were being honest, if I thought it would work…"

He stared into the distance.

"I'd have done it myself already."

Leah and Dorian exchanged looks. She pet Fludge absent-mindedly.

They didn't really know what to say.

"I don't like her going alone," Dorian told Magnus.

"She'll be fine," Magnus assured him. "Aren't you both always talking about how tough she is? I'm sure she'll survive."

He looked at her.

"Now, Detective Bishop," said Magnus. "Run along and make your arrangements. I'd like to speak with my brother. Alone."

"No way in hell am I leaving the two of you alone together," said Leah.

Dorian gave her a rare smile.

"It's all right, Miss Bishop," he said. "Go. I shall catch up with you later."

"*Miss* Bishop? Not using her title, brother? We haven't come far in the equal rights department, it seems to me."

"How *dare* you insinuate –"

Leah muttered to herself, but made her way to the stairs, Fludge trilling with the joy of standing on her shoulder.

She looked back at the two brothers once, and saw they were engaged in some intense, quiet conversation.

There were things about her selkie partner she would probably never understand, being human.

She made her way up the staircase, her head filled with thoughts of prison breaks, the gloaming, and the monster under your bed.

CHAPTER FOURTEEN

eah's first stop was her house in Faerie, where she dropped Fludge in the back garden.

She watched him scamper around in the sunlight, chirping, and wondered what would happen now that she knew more about him.

"You know, it's strange," she told him, even though she knew he didn't understand. "I thought you'd be able to help us with the case. Turns out I learned more about you instead."

Leah watched him run around the garden in circles.

"I wish you could tell me about where you came from. You've lived in both these worlds. Maybe we'd find the key to this mystery."

Fludge ran over to her. Leah sighed and tickled him under the chin.

It was hard to believe that Fludge – *her* Fludge – cute, harmless – unless you counted the fact that he breathed fire like a dragon – ittle Fludge, might be a dangerous monster.

If not today, then one day.

Soon, perhaps.

"Something tried to protect me from you once," she said. "Or something very like you."

Fludge ran off to sniff at the grass.

"Bye for now," she said. "I don't think you'll be safe where I'm going. But I'll come back safe and sound. I promise."

Fludge's attention was elsewhere, engrossed with the petals of a puffy flower.

Leah decided it was the best time to sneak away, before he noticed she was gone.

***

"You want me to what now?"

After Leah had returned Fludge to her home in Faerie, she

and Dorian sought out Aonghas to ask him for another favour.

He did not react well to this request.

The faerie stared at Leah and Dorian as if they had gone insane.

"Please, Aonghas," said Leah. "It's the only way."

"Ben signed –"

"I don't care what Ben signed!" Aonghas exclaimed. "You've already gone back in time once this week, *and* we're still trying to retrieve Dylan. Now Leah wants to go back in time *alone*, and try to convince you hard-headed idiots there's something strange going on in the future? That's it? *That's* the plan?"

"Aonghas –" Leah began, but Aonghas waved her away.

"Don't you *Aonghas* me," he muttered. "So Ben's signed off on this insanity. I certainly hope you have some idea what you're doing. Never mind, obviously you don't, or you wouldn't be doing it."

"What are you so afraid of?" asked Leah.

"That I won't be able to bring you back!" said Aonghas. "It's always a danger, but Leah, you're *human*. If you get trapped, you're not immortal like Dorian, you wouldn't be able to wait it out. You'll age and die just like any human would, stuck in the wrong time period."

"So I won't get stuck," said Leah, with far more bravado than she felt. "Promise."

"You can't promise that."

"Since when do you care what we do, anyway?" Dorian demanded.

Aonghas threw his hands in the air in utter frustration.

"I don't," he said. "But now a Guardian's gone missing and that was my own stupid mistake, so forgive me if I don't have the utmost confidence in my powers at the moment!"

Leah laid a hand on his arm. Aonghas looked at it, and then up at her.

"Well, I do," she said. "You'll find Dylan again, and you won't leave me high and dry. Come on, Aonghas. Please? For me?"

"I have no reason to want to do this *for you* than I would for anyone else," Aonghas grumped. "I'm not the Minotaur. But fine. I'll do it, because Ben signed, not because I think it's in *any way* a good idea."

"Your concerns are noted," said Dorian. "Now, then."

"You know what? I like the girl more."

"Good," said Dorian. "She's the one travelling."

Aonghas turned to Leah.

"Ready?" he asked. She nodded.

"You take care of Fludge while I'm gone, okay?" she told Dorian. "And stay away from your brother!"

Dorian bowed.

"All right, I'm ready," said Leah, steeling herself. "Ready as I'll ever be, anyway."

"Very well," said Aonghas. "I'll come to fetch you in a week."

"What if I haven't found anything?"

"One week, Detective Bishop."

"Okay," said Leah. "One week."

"Don't go getting any strange ideas back there," said Aonghas. "It can do funny things to your mind, time-travel."

Leah nodded.

"Understood," she said. "Now, can you stop waffling and get on with it?"

Aonghas blinked at her, and then uttered a long-suffering sigh.

"As you say," he said, and reached out a hand, lightning playing beneath his palms.

A moment later, a bright flash blinded her. The last thing she saw was Dorian's dark eyes, and his wave of farewell.

***

Leah opened her eyes.

She found herself standing in a smoky back alleyway.

It had just rained. The cobblestones were bright with it.

"Did it work?" she murmured to herself.

She stood up just as a group of guys with gelled-up hairdos

slinked past. One of them wolf-whistled at her.

"Wow," she said, as she surveyed the scene in front of her.

Buchanan Street was a busy place most days, but now it was teeming with people. There was music and a chill in the air. Everyone was dressed to the nines in vintage fashion, but Leah had to remind herself it was current, if Aonghas's aim had been correct – and this time, it looked like it had.

She marvelled at the well-dressed men, the women in heels and stockings, the children in flatcaps bundled up in winter clothing. There was ice slush on the ground, so it must be mid-winter. Belatedly, she registered the reason music was filling the air.

"It's Christmas," she said, and wondered why Aonghas had sent her back to this particular time of year. The first attack of the Gorbals Vampire had been in the summertime, in June.

"Aim's a little off after all, Aonghas," muttered Leah, and walked down the street, hands jammed in her pockets and a little hunched over to ward off the cold.

Someone threw something at the ground beneath her feet, and it pinged off the pavement.

Reaching down, she saw a coin sparkling up at her from the snow.

"Buy yourself some coffee, dear," said an old woman passing by.

"I – but I'm not homeless," Leah called after her. The old woman looked at her doubtfully over her shoulder.

"If you say so," she said. "Buy yourself a coffee anyway, you look chilled to the bone. Happy Christmas."

"Happy Christmas," Leah said in a faltering voice. She stared down at her leather jacket and jeans. Comparatively, she supposed she did look underdressed, particularly for a woman of this time period.

Then she stared at the money in her hand.

"Shillings," she said. *Shit.* Her money wouldn't do her much good here, homeless or not.

And if she was going to be honest, she technically *was* homeless, at least for the time being. Since it was also winter, and not summer as she had expected, that meant she would need to befriend Dorian even more quickly than she had anticipated.

So she had better get a move on.

She hurried down the street to the St. Enoch subway station. By her time, it had been converted to a coffee shop, but it was still the subway station now. She ran around to the back and rubbed her hands together to warm them up before placing her palm against the red sandstone.

"Man, I hope this works," said Leah, "because otherwise, I am in for it."

Nothing happened at first, and her heart tried to claw its way out of her throat.

She took a deep breath and tried to relax. Then she put her hands underneath her shirt and warmed them up on her stomach.

"Come on," she cajoled the wall. "You'll open for vampires, but not for me? They've gotta have colder hands than that."

Leah was acutely aware that people were staring at her curiously as they passed her by.

Still, there was nothing for it, and people in Glasgow had always been a little weird.

It was a big city, after all.

"Here goes nothing," said Leah, and she reached out, pressing her palm against the wall again.

This time, she saw a faint light begin to glow around it, and she almost shouted with joy, but didn't want to jinx it.

There was a loud creak she wasn't used to hearing.

Then, a door swung open in the wall, revealing the familiar long corridor covered in leaves and flowers, where tiny lights giggled from beneath the green.

"Oh, thank God," said Leah, and she slipped in behind the door, which swung closed on a groan behind her.

The warmth of Caledonia Interpol surrounded her, the damp cold leaching out of her bones.

She began to make her way down the staircase, wondering

what she would find at the bottom.

CHAPTER FIFTEEN

er respite from the cold was short-lived. Leah was shocked at the chill when she entered the station.

"Brr!" she said. "What the hell? Did they let the fire go out?"

She walked into the cavernous Great Hall, which still had the look of an ancient library, but now it was freezing cold and there were only a few people present. The enormous fireplace was empty, with only some ashes in the grate to prove it had ever been used for its intended purpose. The firedogs were nowhere to be seen.

It was as unlike her own time as it was possible to be.

But still – there sat Chief Ben in an overcoat and a hat behind his desk. He was smoking a huge cigar while he typed out reports.

Leah glanced upwards and saw it was a cloudy day in the station. Given the lack of bustling people and a working fireplace like she was accustomed to, she wondered if it had any effect on the weather.

"Ah, there you are," said Ben, catching sight of her, "Aoife's swamped. I thought they'd never send somebody from the secretarial pool."

Leah gave him a withering look.

"Say that again and you'll be wearing your face backwards," she told him.

"Ah, a feisty dame," said Ben.

"Did you just –" Leah sighed and backtracked. "Okay, I don't know how else to do this, don't really have any practise, but I – I'm from the future."

Ben's finger clicked at one letter of his typewriter as he stared back at her.

"Pardon?" he said.

She walked up to his desk and sat down in front of him.

"I'm one of your employees, from the future," she said. "Detective Inspector Leah Bishop. And I'm here because one of your old cases has come around again."

"Detective?" said Ben, peering at her. His brows drew together. "But – you're *human*?"

"Yeah," said Leah.

"Why would I hire a human?" Ben asked.

"You got me," she said, suddenly enjoying herself very much. "'Cause I'm just that good, I guess."

"Well, you got in here somehow," he said. "And the wall wouldn't have opened if you weren't in my employ. Can't hurt to indulge you, I suppose. What can I do for you, Detective?"

"First of all, where's your security?" asked Leah. "Second, where's the heat?"

Ben sighed. He leaned back and put his hands behind his head, puffing at his cigar.

"They cut our budget the last few years," he said. "I figured Caledonia Interpol was on its way out. Just crossing some t's and dotting some i's before the inevitable. Now here you are, darkening my doorway. If you're from the future, and it's better then, you've given me the best hope I've had in decades."

"You better not say *she was brunette, and dangerous,* next," said Leah.

"Wouldn't dream of it," he said. "Why do you –"

Leah waved it away.

"Never mind, it's not important," she said. "Anyway, we're looking into the vampire with iron teeth again."

"The one the kids have been saying terrorised the cemetery?" asked Ben, leaning forward. "I hate to disappoint you after coming all this way, but we don't really think there's anything to it. We've looked into it and as far as we can tell, it's just a bunch of children reading too many American comic books."

"And whose mums and dads sing them to sleep with *Jenny wi' the Airn Teeth*?" asked Leah.

Ben paused.

"You think it's something the children have manifested?" he asked. "That would explain a lot."

Leah shrugged.

"Kids and animals can see things we can't," she said. "They believe, harder than just about anybody. A bunch of them all start believing in the same thing at the same time, who knows what could happen? Child lore survives because of how quickly stories and songs spread among children, passed down from older child to younger, and that's been true forever. So –"

" – their propensity for storytelling and belief would create a horrible monster indeed," finished Ben. "But one, perhaps, that only children can see?"

"That's the current working theory."

Ben regarded her with a different air.

"You *are* good," he said.

"Like I said," Leah told him, "that's why you hired me."

"Hmm," said Ben, "I shall have to make a note of this for the future. Where'd you come from?"

"I was a regular human police officer, in Edinburgh," she said. "But I'm from Glasgow, originally. Before I joined the police, I'd trained as a folklorist."

Ben nodded, jotting it down on a piece of paper.

"Does that mean –"

"What?" asked Ben.

"Well, did you hire me then or just remind yourself to hire me now?" asked Leah. "And if so, how did you know to hire me the first time?"

"Time-travel, my dear," said Ben, until he noticed Leah glaring daggers at him and amended, "Detective. It's best not to ask how these things are – not ours to wonder why, and so forth."

"I take issue with the *do or die* aspect of the rest of that quote," said Leah, "but point taken."

"Who did I partner you with?" he asked. "It couldn't have been somebody else new, that wouldn't make much sense for a human recruit to the monster police."

"Dorian Grey."

There was a dead silence from Ben.

He looked at her carefully.

"Did you say *Dorian* Grey?" he asked.

"Yes, I'd like to work with him again, if that would be all right."

"Are you sure you wouldn't rather work with his brother, Magnus? He's –"

"No!" barked Leah, with a little more force than she intended. She recovered slightly. "It's just, Dorian and me. We, er. We work well together."

"If you say so," said Ben. "I just don't think – well, if you're sure."

"I'm sure," said Leah. "He's a brilliant detective."

Ben narrowed his eyes.

"And you two are – close, are you?"

"He's my best friend."

Leah really, really wanted to know the reason Ben was staring at her as if she had three heads.

"Aoife," called Ben, and Leah was thrilled to see the same tattooed receptionist she had come to know in her time period, dressed to the absolute nines in a bright red dress and a perfect hairdo, "Can you call Dorian in here?"

Aoife's smile faltered. She paused.

"Are you –" she said, her eyes drifting over to Leah. "Are you quite sure it's *Dorian* you want, Chief?"

"Leah here is from the future," said Ben. "Apparently she works with us, and Dorian's her partner. *Apparently.*"

Aoife's smile dropped another notch.

"Dorian *Grey,* that is?" she asked.

Ben nodded. They seemed to have a silent conversation.

"Whatever you say, Chief," she said, and disappeared.

Leah watched her go, then turned back to Ben.

"What *is* it with everybody?" asked Leah. "Is there something wrong with Dorian?"

"You called, Chief?" said a voice.

Leah turned around to see a slight man in a fedora.

He stumbled a little, catching himself against the wall.

He looked up, bright brown eyes gleaming with mischief.

And inebriation, more likely than not.

"Dorian Grey," he said, nodding to Leah. "At your service."

CHAPTER SIXTEEN

Who's the dame?"

Dorian lit a cigarette and gazed coolly at Leah from under the brim of his fedora.

"Your new partner," said Ben.

Dorian shot him a look.

"I work alone," he groused. "Or with Magnus if he needs help. You know that."

"Seems that I, in my infinite wisdom, paired you up with her," said Ben. "In the future."

Dorian gave Leah the once-over.

"Time-traveller, eh?" he asked with a wink. "They sure build 'em sturdy in the future – wait. Boss, she's human!"

"She is," said Leah. "And in the future, she's your partner."

"Since when did we start recruiting humans?" asked Dorian.

"Long story, can't share, you understand," snarked Leah.

"Aw, c'mon, boss, you can't –"

"I did it once before. Or I will in the future."

"And you trust that?"

"Yeah, I trust me," said Ben.

"I'm here for a good time, not for a long time," said Leah.

"Hey, that's good! That's very good. You say things like that in the future?" Dorian shook his head. "She got a mouth on her, don't she."

Leah just stared at him.

"You're – not the same," said Leah.

"Times change, doll," said Dorian.

"You call me that again, I put your teeth on the other side of your skull."

"And you say two are close?" ventured Ben. "In the future?"

"Best friends, actually," said Leah.

"Bosom companions," said Dorian, angling a look at her chest.

This time, she really did punch him.

Dorian rubbed his cheek, a newfound respect dawning in his eyes.

"You know," he said. "I don't know whether to kiss her or kill her. C'mon, sweetheart, I'll buy you a drink. Let's get reacquainted."

Leah rolled her eyes.

"So you'll help in her investigation, then?" asked Ben.

"Sure thing, Chief," said Dorian, throwing his cigarette into the barren fireplace. "You know me, always willing to lend a hand, a friend to all. Ready?"

Dorian offered the crook of his elbow to Leah, who took it, more amused by the minute.

"Great," sighed Ben, as he watched them walk out of the office. "I had one wildcard. Now I have two."

***

Leah was surprised to note that while the pub catering to the local monster police wasn't called Waxy's, since it hadn't been opened yet, it was in the same location.

"You do drink, right?" asked Dorian, leaning forward in the press of bodies surrounded by a fug of smoke in the bar.

"Yeah," said Leah.

"What's your poison?"

"Single malt. Neat."

"Hey Charlie. Two whiskies, neat."

"Comin' right up."

"Don't you want to know what kind?" asked Leah.

Dorian gave her a puzzled look.

"There's just the one?" he hazarded.

"Now that can't be true," she said.

"Oh, sure, there's all kinds of distilleries," he told her. "But you want to get your hands on the fine stuff, you're paying top dollar. And sure as hell not in a copper's pub like this one."

Leah smiled softly.

"You know, we have a place like this in my time," she said.

"We used to go – but. Well. Not these days."

Dorian took the glasses and set them down at a corner table.

"Something happen between the two of you?" he asked. "Between – us?"

Leah nodded, wrapping her hand around the whisky glass.

"Too much to tell," she said.

"Right," said Dorian. "Time travel. Can't give anything away." He took a sip.

"Why are you –" Leah sipped the whisky. It was rough. "Fuck! This is like drinking glass shards."

"Water of life," said Dorian. "You drink it, you know you're not dead."

"But you wish you were."

"You were saying?"

"Just –" she waved a hand at Dorian's getup, at Dorian in general. "I thought – well. You were Taken, you became the perfect man for Dahlia, all trussed up in waistcoats, Victorian stick up your arse, that kind of thing."

Leah blinked at the whisky. Dorian winked at her.

"What'd I say?" he said. "Tastes like rubbish, but gets the job done."

"Faster than usual, I'd expect."

"I take it you're not usually a cheap date."

"Hell no. Dorian – my Dorian, from my time – only made the mistake of offering to buy once. Nearly had to pay for the entire bar's worth of whisky. We've gone Dutch ever since."

"Well, either they've refined things in your day, or you'll still be formidable in mine," said Dorian, grinning.

Leah stared at the grin, mystified.

"I like a dame who speaks her mind, knows how to fight. A bit of rough."

"Yes, Dahlia was that kind of woman," said Leah.

"I seem to have told you all my tragic little stories."

"Some, yes. Others, no. Kind of – kind of how we got into the trouble we've been having."

"Well, to answer your question, after I was Taken, I did become something of the upstanding young gentleman in society," said Dorian. "For Dahlia's sake. But Dahlia's gone, and I take it you also know that I wasn't always the perfect specimen of repressed Victorian manhood?"

Leah grinned.

"Yes, we worked a case," she said, "where you reverted, shall we say, to your old personality. I did not know there were so many different varieties of opium."

"Or so many ways to enjoy the evening with so many different kinds of men," said Dorian, finishing his whisky. "Or women, or other. I didn't really see the difference between them. Never have, never will."

Leah glanced around the room.

"Should you be saying things like that, right out in public?" asked Leah. "I don't know much about this time period, but I'm pretty sure it's not safe."

Dorian nodded at the crowd around the bar.

"This place is a pub for the monster police," he said. "Monsters don't care about things like that."

"Wow, I thought the numbers had dwindled," said Leah. "I saw hardly anybody at the office."

"Who spends time at the office?" asked Dorian. "It's freezing, for one. Ben gets saddled with a mountain of paperwork, so he has to be there, although where he sends it to after filling it out is still a mystery to me. Say, have you ever found out who runs Interpol? Or come to that, who started it? Caledonia is only one office. There are several throughout the world."

"You know," said Leah, finishing her whisky, "I've never really thought about it."

"That amazes me," said Dorian. "We talk about it all the time."

"Sounds like the officers are close."

"Aren't they, in your time?"

"Things change."

Dorian lit a cigarette and nodded.

"Indeed."

"My shout," said Leah, and she went up to the bar.

Her mind was spinning. This Dorian was so calm and collected, so *cool,* like he'd stepped right out of a film noir. And he was *talkative,* for want of a better word. These officers spent most of their time outdoors. They were doing active police work in the dark and dingy alleyways of Glasgow, walking through the mist-filled streets.

Leah felt far more at home here.

As she paid and ferried the drinks back over to the table, she had a sudden wistful longing she would never have predicted.

A part of her wanted to stay.

She really felt like she fit in better, in this far more active Glasgow, back in the day when they still patrolled the streets.

Besides…

This Dorian was so easy to talk to. He was so *different,* but familiar all the same. It was like getting her best friend back again, but without all that history.

Leah had never felt like she fit at Caledonia Interpol. Partly because she was human, partly because she missed the days spent walking the beat.

There was a reason the word *gumshoe* had come from this earlier, simpler time.

"So," he said, as she returned. "Ben tells me there's a problem with the 'vampire with iron teeth' at the Southern Necropolis?"

Leah nodded, getting comfortable in her chair.

"Yeah," she said. "We've done some investigation. The Fae underworld, the Goblin Market."

Dorian whistled.

"You *are* a tough cookie," he said, impressed.

Leah had to bite the inside of her cheek to stop herself from laughing at the comment.

"So the working theory is that this creature isn't Fae, not really," said Leah. "But something created by the minds of children."

"Interesting," said Dorian, leaning in. "We had assumed it was because of the children reading too many American comic books and dropped it. None of our vampire contacts had ever heard anything about this vampire."

"We thought the same thing," said Leah. "But kids are disappearing. According to the other children, at least, even though we're not seeing any reports of missing children. Something's taking them."

"And you're certain it's not human?" asked Dorian.

"Yeah," said Leah. "We've had intel from informants in three different time periods, and I was sent to this one because they wanted it straight from the horse's mouth, so to speak."

"Have you considered that what the children are seeing might not be other children at all?"

Leah sat up.

"No," she said. "We've been so focused on what the monster might be that we hadn't thought about whether the children might be something else too."

"It stands to reason that if a monster can be invented, so too can the victims," said Dorian. "It'd explain why there have been no missing persons cases filed."

"Every time I think I've got a lead, it just gets weirder," said Leah. "Say that's true. What could it be? What could disguise itself as children? And what kind of monster would be interested in kidnapping these…not-children?"

"I confess, I have no idea," he said. "But it's worth considering."

"Any wild guesses?"

Dorian smoked, and drank his whisky; he thought about it, and offered various solutions, leads that Leah hadn't thought about or had already passed on for several reasons. Leah asked him questions and discussed the aspects of Faerie that might have led to the manifestation of a creature in the cemetery.

Or what may have led to a manifestation of things that looked like children but were not children.

After a while, Leah was startled to discover that she was *happy*.

They were playing off each other again, each using the other's intellect and knowledge to hone their investigation to a fine point. Leah had forgotten how much she missed it, how they had always moved together in a kind of intricate dance.

And it was so *easy.*

Easy as falling.

This is great, thought Leah. *Just like old times.*

CHAPTER SEVENTEEN

When they left the bar later that night, Leah was far past tipsy and straight into drunk.

More surprisingly, so was Dorian.

This was a first for Leah, in all the time she had known him.

"You know," he slurred, as they walked into the Glasgow gloom together, "most humans can't keep up with the Fae where drinking is concerned."

"I can't believe you got that entire sentence out of your mouth," said Leah. "But you learned that wasn't always true, and you learned fast, when you met me."

They leaned against each other, and Leah was smiling so hard it hurt.

"Huh," she said, looking around herself. "City hasn't changed much."

Walking through the Trongate wasn't so different.

There was the same orange-golden light, the chill air, the darkness, the *flavour* of the night she tasted was the same.

"I feel I'd know Glasgow by scent alone," nodded Dorian. "The city may not be Paris or Rome, but in its own way, it is eternal."

Leah nodded.

"Ain't that the truth," she said.

This, this companionable perfection –

Leah had missed this, or maybe never really had it, with the Dorian of her time.

"This is great," she said. "Really wonderful. It's good to hang out with you again."

"Yes, I can see how we became such close companions in the future," Dorian agreed. "We have much in common."

"Well," said Leah, pausing. "In the future – not exactly."

"Oh?" asked Dorian, puzzled. "Then why?"

"Honestly?" said Leah. "*Because* we're different, except in the ways where it counts. Loyalty. Love, I guess."

She didn't say *and it was that same foolish loyalty that caused a crack in the foundation I don't know if we can ever repair.*

"Say," Dorian said. "I wonder if you'd be a good match for my brother, Magnus. You haven't mentioned him, have you not met?"

Leah choked a little.

"Er, yeah, we've met," she said. "Not my type."

"Magnus is everyone's type," sighed Dorian. "Are you sure he–"

There was a loud clang from a side alley.

Dorian and Leah straightened up, the conversation blessedly forgotten.

"What was that?" she asked, sobering a little.

"Beats me," Dorian answered. "But we're the police, so."

"Monster police," Leah reminded him.

Dorian gave her a look out of the corner of his big brown eyes.

"Police are police, Leah," he said. "We go where we're needed."

"Huh," said Leah again, and followed Dorian down the alleyway.

***

There was a woman at the end of the alley who had collapsed onto the ground in the fog.

"Ma'am?" asked Dorian. "Are you all right?"

The woman mumbled something.

"Drunk?" ventured Leah.

"No, I don't think so," said Dorian, squatting down in front of her. "Ma'am?"

"Just – give me a few minutes," mumbled the woman.

"What you need is three squares and somewhere to lay your head," Dorian declared. "Here, come on, let's help her up."

Leah and Dorian got their arms underneath her and helped her to stand.

"There's a soup kitchen down the street," he said. "Let's go."

When they handed her over to the woman in charge of the soup kitchen, she smiled.

"You're angels, bringing her here," she said. "Not many would. We don't live in good times, and it's just so easy to ignore."

"All part of a night's work, ma'am," said Dorian, sliding a finger around the brim of his hat.

He walked out into the street with Leah.

"Now, where can I drop you?" he asked.

"Er," said Leah. "I don't think anyone thought this far ahead." Dorian stared at her.

"They let you time-travel...homeless?" he asked.

"Yeah. You may as well leave me at the soup kitchen too," said Leah.

"Nonsense," said Dorian. "My best friend? I don't think the future version of myself would thank me for that. No, you're coming home with me."

"Home?" asked Leah, confused. "You have a *home*?"

"Doesn't everyone?" asked Dorian. "Don't tell me I've never invited you over? My own best friend?"

"Things have been," said Leah, "er. Stilted, of late."

"But even before?"

"Honestly," said Leah, "it never came up. In our time period, it's not that common. Besides, I assumed you had some selkie reason for it."

"Selkies are homely," said Dorian. "That's part of our charm. Making a good nest for those we love and all that."

"Oh," said Leah. "Then I wonder –"

"Well," said Dorian. "I'm sure he had his reasons. Just as I have mine. Come on."

He crooked his arm toward her, and she took it.

And to Leah's startled surprise, she walked arm in arm with her best friend through the streets of Glasgow.

***

151

Dorian's house was...

not what Leah had expected.

Truth be told, she wasn't sure what she'd expected.

"You live here?" she asked.

"Why?" asked Dorian. "You expected something more?"

The two-bedroom flat overlooked the Clyde.

It looked just like every other flat she had ever seen in the city, and dingier than most.

"I thought..." she began. "Well. I know how rich you both are, and I thought..."

Dorian grinned.

"It'd be something a bit more ostentatious?" he asked.

She nodded.

"Well, I don't deny we have money," said Dorian. "But we have to live a bit under our means, should we wish to keep it."

"Okay, but...something a little better than this?" said Leah.

"I can see water outside my window," Dorian shrugged. "That's all I need, a reminder of, a connection to, the sea. You want to see ostentation, you ought to see where Magnus –"

"No!" said Leah, a bit louder than intended.

Now Dorian was really looking at her strangely.

"All right," he said. "I understand your reasoning for not telling me anything about the future, but there's something wrong with Magnus, isn't there?"

Leah's mouth snapped shut.

"Yes, I understand you don't want to tell me," said Dorian. "Or maybe you can't. But I think – in fact, it is his night off. Let's go and see him, shall we?"

"Dorian," Leah warned.

"You can tell me, or not tell me," said Dorian. "But I'd like to introduce you, either way. So either you tell me now, or we go to Magnus's place."

Leah crossed her arms, resolute.

Dorian opened the door again and ushered her into the hall-way.

"You're such an arse when you want to get your way," complained Leah.

"Some things never change," Dorian said, and was off down the hall before Leah had time to think, making her run to catch up.

***

Back outside, the shadows of the city had deepened.

The streets were bare of people, as it was after bar close.

Dorian's steps led them into the fanciest part of Merchant City, where he finally stopped in front of an unassuming door.

The selkie paused a moment before knocking.

"Last chance," said Dorian. "Tell me, or we meet him."

"That's a hell of a threat," said Leah. "I'm not a suspect, Dorian! There's no need for the third degree. And you know I can't tell you. Even if I wanted to, and believe me, I do! Why are you so stupid when it comes to your brother, anyway?"

"Hm," said Dorian, and he turned to knock on the door.

Leah's thoughts went from desperate to panicked. She didn't know how to get out of the situation. She kicked herself for not planning ahead, and not keeping a poker face where Magnus was concerned.

But she hadn't, so now here she was, and she knew just how determined and stubborn her best friend and partner could be.

The door swung open, revealing a maid in a French-maid-style uniform.

She was even carrying a feather duster.

"Yes?" she enquired politely.

Music and laughter floated down the staircase.

"Oh, hello, Dorian," she said.

"Time's up," Dorian told Leah, and turned to the woman in the doorway. "Hello, Celeste. We're here to see my brother."

"Oh, he'll be delighted!" she said. "He's having a party. He's invited you many times, Dorian."

"Aye, I know," said Dorian. "This is my new partner, Leah. May we come in?"

"Of course," said Celeste, turning to the side to let them through. "You know the way? Would you like me to escort you?"

"No need to stand on ceremony for us," said Dorian.

He looked at Leah.

"Coming?" he asked.

He held out his elbow for her.

Leah stared up the staircase and sighed.

She linked arms with him, and they made their way upstairs.

CHAPTER EIGHTEEN

The door opened at the top of the staircase, and there he stood.

Beautiful. Incredible.

And deadly, thought Leah, as the familiar wave of selkie magic washed over her.

"Dorian!" Magnus exclaimed, hugging his brother. "Delighted you finally decided to grace us with your presence."

Then he caught sight of Leah.

"Well hello," he purred. "And who's this?"

"This is my new partner, Leah," said Dorian. "Ben assigned her to me, believe it or not."

Magnus raised a perfectly arched eyebrow.

"*Partner?*" he repeated. "And you allowed that?"

"Don't you think that charm's a little over the top, brother?" asked Dorian, nodding in Magnus's general direction. "There's a reason humans dislike it when a man wears too much cologne."

"Oh, this?" asked Magnus airily. "It's just for the party."

"Magnus."

"Oh, very well," said Magnus, and the powerful sense of attraction Leah felt began to diminish.

"Charmed to make your acquaintance," said Magnus, holding out his hand.

Leah smiled but did not reach out.

After a moment, Magnus retracted his hand.

"Won't you both come in," said Magnus, giving Leah an odd look but nevertheless ushering them inside.

Leah barged forward into the crowd, so she didn't have to be near Magnus any more than necessary.

She cursed herself. This wasn't how things were supposed to go! How was she meant to keep such an incredible secret to herself? When she could actually *save* people, if she just told Dorian the truth?

"All right, that's it," said Dorian, storming up to her. "That was incredibly rude. Explain yourself."

"I already told you, I can't say," said Leah. "And you forced me to come here, even *after* I told you it was a bad idea!"

Leah was sour to the heart as she realised the fights had started again –

Dorian, always believing he was in the right.

Leah, unable to watch her mouth just to keep the peace.

Maybe, she thought, it was inevitable, and their friendship would always come down to this, no matter the time period.

"Okay," she sighed. "You want to know?"

"I really do."

"Then on your head be it," said Leah.

She took a deep breath, steeling herself.

"Magnus is a murderer," she told Dorian. "In the future, yes, but also in the past. You saw him – or you thought you saw him – throw the body of your Taken lover into the Thames in London. But you kept it to yourself, because you couldn't be certain, because you loved drugs more than you loved anything, and because you were such a useless fuck in those days that if you lost Magnus, you didn't know what you were going to do. And knowing what I know – that your brother is imprisoned in the Deeps of Interpol – and knowing the things he did, Dorian, I thought I could – but I can't. Okay?"

Dorian stared at her.

"Are you going to tell me or not?" he demanded.

Leah stared back at him.

"What the hell do you mean?" she said. "I just did!"

"You didn't say a word," said Dorian. "You just stood there, looking at me."

"I swear I told you," she said. Dorian shook his head.

"Your brother is a serial killer!" she shouted.

She turned around and looked at the crowd, dancing and making merry all around her.

"Hey!" she bellowed. "Magnus Grey is a murderer! I have proof!"

But no one reacted at all, not even to look over at the noise she was making.

"Leah?" prompted Dorian.

"Look, I keep *trying*," she said in frustration. "But I just yelled at the crowd, and nobody even reacted."

"Hm," said Dorian. "Maybe it's a kind of, I don't know, protection spell? That Caledonia put on anyone who time-travels. To keep people from blabbing."

"Seems likely," said Leah. "And if that's the case, are you gonna believe me now that I *can't tell you*? Just trust me when I say *I don't like your brother.*"

"Well, that's a little unfair, isn't it?" came a silky voice at her shoulder, making her jump. "And you haven't even tried my cocktails."

Magnus stood there, holding a wine glass in one hand, and looking from one to the other of them with amusement.

The way he said *cocktails* with that salacious grin made Leah want to punch the double-entendre right off his face.

"We've had a lot to drink," said Dorian, stepping smoothly between his brother and Leah. "Care to bring us more?"

"Certainly," said Magnus, lathering his words with charm. "Perhaps I can convince your lovely partner to give me a second chance?"

"She only drinks whisky," said Dorian.

"A pity," said Magnus.

The implication dripped from his words that Leah's taste was the pity. His tone made it clear he wouldn't allow such low-end swill in his house.

"Aside from cocktails, all we have is high-end pink champagne."

"We'll both take a glass of champagne," said Dorian. "Magnus. Please."

"As you say," Magnus said, and drifted off toward the drinks table.

"I don't know what it is that Magnus has done," said Dorian, turning to Leah, "but please, be civil! For both our sakes."

"Fine," grumped Leah. "Can't say he'd butter me up with that condescending tone about whisky, either way."

Dorian shrugged.

"Most people see it as uncouth, these days," said Dorian. "The only people who drink it are drunks and coppers, unless you can get your hands on the good stuff."

"In my time, it's some of the most expensive alcohol available," said Leah.

"That...seems unlikely."

"Oh, so it's okay for you to hear *that* completely useless information about the future," she groused. "Anyway. I'll do my best."

Magnus returned, holding two delicate crystal glasses with sparkling pink liquid, and handed them off to Leah and Dorian.

"Now, then," Magnus said politely. "What is it you do for Caledonia Interpol?"

"More than you," she mumbled into her glass.

"What was that?" asked Magnus.

"She's from the future," said Dorian. "She's here investigating the vampire with the iron teeth. Seems to be a repeating problem."

"What?" asked Magnus. "I thought we'd decided it was just children with overactive imaginations."

"That may, in itself, be the issue," said Dorian.

"Oh," said Magnus. Then, "*Oh!* Something created by children?"

"Stories have to come from somewhere."

"This is quite the breakthrough in the case," said Magnus. "I can join you tomorrow, if you like."

"Won't you be hungover?" asked Leah, trying to modulate her tone.

Magnus gave her a look.

"Won't you?"

He appeared to mull things over.

"On second thought, how about I join you right now? What's the next step?"

"That's quite all right, Magnus, we can work alone –" said Dorian, clearly alarmed at this development, particularly where Leah's interests were concerned.

"Nonsense," said Magnus, already going for his coat. "Ben's told you for years you can't keep working alone, no matter how much you want to. He's tried to partner the two of us up, ever since we were first hired – and, well. I'm glad to see you're working with someone else, but frankly, Dorian, she's human and doesn't have the senses we do."

"You want to leave the party? Now?" asked Dorian, gesturing at all the people in the room.

"Oh, sure," he said. "These people? They don't care about me at all. Won't even notice I'm gone. This is a longstanding weekly party, sometimes I do extra ones, anyway I doubt they'd notice if I died."

He waved a hand at the crowd. No one responded; they were too involved in their own conversations, or the drinks table.

"That's..." said Leah, and paused. "Kind of sad."

"Well, what can you do? People are selfish. They value money and good times over everything else," said Magnus. "Now, where are we off to, Dorian?"

"It's late," said Dorian. "We need to get rest sometime soon, Magnus. Selkies or not, we need sleep."

"We can sleep when we're seals," Magnus replied. "What's the use of selkie magic if we can't employ it to help other people?"

He shrugged his coat over his shoulders.

"I don't know about you, but I'd like to take another look at that graveyard."

He opened the door and looked over his shoulder at them.

"Well?"

Dorian glanced at Leah, then shook his head in apology and followed his brother.

Leah grit her teeth, bit her tongue, and trailed the two selkies back outside into the Glasgow night.

CHAPTER NINETEEN

So, Leah and I were apparently caught at the greengrocer's, pursued by some kind of horrific creature that was half-human, half-spider," Dorian finished filling his brother in on the situation.

"And she and I don't get along in the future for some reason she can't tell you."

"Apparently."

Leah wanted to say *both our future and your past,* but by this point understood it was useless. Whatever magic allowed time-travel wouldn't let her voice it. So she was going to have to work with both selkie-men as if it were any other case.

Taking a deep breath, she ploughed onward:

"And if the children of *this* time period created a monster because they were sung *Jenny wi' the airn teeth,* we need to find out how it began, go to the source and see if we can stop it from happening."

"If it's something children have created in their collective consciousness, preventing it would be unlikely," reasoned Magnus. "We'd have to stop the man from writing the song in the first place."

"Can we do that?"

"Maybe," Dorian said. "But the song became popular for a reason. We get rid of that one, another one just springs up in its place."

"And children have powerful imaginations."

"*Keep away from children* is sounding a lot more like good advice than just something they write on plastic bags," Leah commented.

Both brothers glanced at each other, and then her.

"What?" they asked in chorus.

"Nothing. Future stuff," said Leah, waving them off. "If you could hear it, then it wasn't important."

They were approaching the Southern Necropolis now. The

cemetery was overgrown but beautiful, peaceful in its own way. Large trees overhung the gravestones and gave an air of sombre sentimentality to the place.

"I don't know what we'll be able to learn from the graveyard," said Leah. "If only children can see this thing, then I think we're out of luck."

"You never know," said Magnus. "There are always clues, no matter the crime."

Leah hated to admit that despite Magnus's many sins, he was a good detective.

Dorian walked into the graveyard on his own, examining the moss-covered headstones and the damp earth, leaving them alone together.

"So what was it?" asked Magnus, hands in his pockets against the late-night Glasgow chill, as the mist twined through the cemetery and Dorian knelt to study the inscriptions on the weather-worn stone. "What did I do to you? One-night stand? Leave you high and dry?"

Leah barked a laugh.

"You wish," she said.

"Or a friend of yours?" he guessed.

She steeled herself, knowing whatever magic was watching over her would not let her tell the truth, and put all the vitriol she could into a single word.

"Murderer," she snarled.

Magnus stared at her.

His face drained of colour.

"How did you –" he began.

Leah stared back at him.

"You – you heard that?" she asked, horrified.

"Please, for the love of God, don't tell my brother," Magnus begged.

"Already tried. The magic won't let me," said Leah. "But *you* seemed to hear me just fine."

"Leah, hear me out."

"I'm not sure you deserve that, but do I have another choice?"

162

"This – it's about Dahlia, right?" asked Magnus hurriedly. "The – the torso they found. They blamed it on the Ripper. Somebody saw me, they must have – how else would you know? Does Dorian –"

"*Dorian saw you*," Leah hissed.

Magnus glanced over at his brother.

"Then why –"

"He was so fucking high at the time he couldn't be sure," said Leah. "Besides. He depended on you, back then. So he kept his mouth shut. He knew which side his bread was buttered on."

"Leah. Please let me explain."

"You've got about a minute before Dorian comes back over here."

"Dahlia was murdered, it's true," Magnus said quickly. "I found her – I – I found what was left of her, anyway. And Dorian, well. I knew if he found her like that, it – he's sensitive, far more sensitive than he lets on, he was even in those days, although it's never been obvious. It would have done something horrible to him."

"And it didn't do something horrible to you?"

"Maybe it did," he admitted. "But in all things, I protect my brother first. I love him. I would have done anything – *anything* for him. *Taking care of Dorian is my job.* I thought it best he believed she had abandoned him, as selkies' lovers often do. Yes, he would suffer the fate of the rejected Taken selk, but – he wouldn't have to know, wouldn't have to see – what I've seen. What I saw that night, and yes, I was the one who put what was left of her in the Thames. But I did not put her there."

"Police only recovered a torso," said Leah. Magnus nodded, and how had she never noticed the horror hiding behind his eyes before tonight?

"It was not," he said, coughing as his voice broke, and she could hear tears brimming in his words, "just a torso, Leah. That may have been all they found, but it – she –"

He blew out a breath, and squeezed his eyes shut, shaking his head against the memories.

"Let's just say, if I hadn't known her well, it would have been impossible to identify," he said, in a more measured tone, "the pieces."

This time a tear did fall.

Then he looked up at her.

"I did not murder her myself," he said, as he looked at the palm of his hand. "But I can still see – sometimes, in the right light – my hands covered with blood."

"Have you," Leah began, wondering if there was some way around the magic, some way to prevent what was to come, "have you considered talking to someone about this? Not Dorian. Someone else. *Anyone* else."

Magnus gave her a little smile.

"Well, I'm talking to you now, aren't I?" he asked.

Dorian returned at that point, effectively ending their conversation.

"I think I may have found something," he said.

Leah and Magnus exchanged glances, and in silent agreement, they consigned their discussion to history.

CHAPTER TWENTY

hat is it?" asked Leah. "What did you find?"

Dorian looked between her and his brother with suspicion, but pressed on.

"You'd mentioned that old song, *Jenny wi' the airn teeth*," said Dorian. Leah nodded. "Well, that song is based on an older folkloric legend. But it's English."

"Do you mean Jenny Greenteeth?" Leah asked.

"Yes," said Dorian.

"What would an English monster be doing all the way up here?" asked Magnus.

"Why are the English *ever* up here?" muttered Dorian.

"What, you think this is some kind of interloper?" asked Leah.

"More like a monster takeover," said Dorian. "Monsters often mirror their origin culture."

"Folklore is shared across these islands," said Leah. "I doubt a single monster could –"

"That's just it," said Dorian. "They come not single spy, but –"

"In battalions," she finished.

***

They took their theory to Chief Ben.

"What evidence do you have of this?" he asked. "Theories are all well and good, Dorian, but really? A monster invasion?"

"What they couldn't do with war, they'll do with money," said Leah. "Money has always flowed south. I don't know how it works with monsters but Dorian's right – these creatures may be higher in number than we'd imagined."

"And what, you think *children* are responsible?" asked Ben, incredulous.

"Not responsible, as such," Magnus cut in, "but *something* is harnessing the awesome power of children's nightmares and turning them real, specifically the *Jenny wi' the airn teeth* myth."

"I don't see how the existence of one or several of these monsters would be particularly detrimental to Scotland and its monster population," said Ben.

"I do," said Leah. "I've seen one."

"You have? Where?"

"At a grocery store, in the future. It came after me and Dorian, but I knocked it out with a jar of clotted cream."

They all looked at her then. She waved her hand at them.

"It was just what I had in my hand at the time, all right?" she said. "Anyway, this thing seemed to be targeting us specifically. A fog came down and it was like we were being hunted."

Now Ben was given pause.

"Monsters hunting monsters," he ruminated. "It's been a very long time since those days."

"And it looks like those days may be returning," said Leah. "Ignoring it during this time period has made the monsters far stronger in mine. I don't know what's going on in Faerie at the moment, but I have a hunch you might be losing monsters left and right very soon."

"Any idea how to stop it, if that's what is happening?"

Leah shrugged.

"All I know about Jenny Greenteeth is that she doesn't like iron," said Leah.

"Most Fae don't like iron."

"I know," sighed Leah. "Guess that's why you hired me in the first place."

***

There wasn't much more Ben could do for them, so he thanked them for their work on the investigation and sent them home, saying they looked exhausted. Magnus made his excuses and left, mentioning he needed to return home and make sure there had been sufficient cleanup after the party.

"Sometimes I think the only one who misses me is Celeste,"

he said with a sad smile. "And sometimes, I'm not even sure about her."

He nodded to them with a wink, and then walked off into the darkness.

"So," said Dorian, as they walked alone together through the last vestiges of another rainy Glasgow night, the puddles reflecting the orange lights of the city. "You're a folklorist, and I have limited contact with the monsters down south. What can you tell me about this one?"

"Well," said Leah, shoving her hands into the pockets of her leather jacket, "Jenny Greenteeth is a river monster. She drowns children and the elderly."

"Why?"

Leah shrugged.

"Just 'cause. Sometimes there isn't a reason."

"Kelpies eat the children, at the very least."

"Yes, Dorian, let's focus on the monster's purpose."

"Apologies. What reason would Jenny Greenteeth, or multiple manifestations of her, have for hunting down and destroying the monsters of Scotland?"

Leah looked out over the city she loved, its red sandstone and its ancient bricks, the strange beauty of the working-class city that had endured over the centuries.

"The thing is," she said slowly, "I don't exactly know why, but I got the distinct impression the creature attacking us at the grocery store wasn't necessarily happy about it? It screamed, which I first thought was an attempt at intimidation, but now I wonder if it was pain."

"Pain?" repeated Dorian. "You think someone is controlling her? All of them?"

Leah nodded.

"In our time," she said, "there is, or was before he was killed, a criminal mastermind of the city named Sebastian. If this were any other time period, I'd say this reminded me of his fingerprint. Now, I couldn't venture to guess, other than the usual *perfidious Albion* motive."

"Doing evil for the sake of doing evil," nodded Dorian. "Yes, I see what you mean. I just cannot imagine the reasoning, or the benefit behind it."

"That's just it, Dorian," said Leah. "Sometimes the motive is just *because I wanted to, and I could.*"

Dorian shivered visibly.

"Those were always the criminals I could never stomach," he said, a faraway look in his eyes.

Leah knew he was thinking of Dahlia then, and of his brother.

It saddened her to know he would have further cause for that look in the future.

But she left her thoughts there, as they had a case to solve.

They climbed up the stairs together and went into Dorian's apartment.

"I'm exhausted," said Dorian. "Feel free to use the guest bedroom, there. I believe the bed is still made up."

"Thank you, Dorian," said Leah, "I might stay up for a little while and think."

"Make yourself at home," Dorian replied, setting his fedora on the table, and shrugging out of the trenchcoat he wore.

The selkie vanished into the back bedroom and closed the door.

Leah stood in the living room, looking out at the Clyde below and the city beyond through the windows of Dorian's humble apartment. She turned her knowledge of Jenny Greenteeth over and over again in her head.

Wicked Jenny. They also call pondweed the same thing because it looks like a surface that could support weight, so it often leads to drowning.

What reason would someone have to hunt Scottish monsters? Why here, why now? Why the Southern Necropolis in particular?

Peg Powler is a similar legend and would explain the fog...

Or maybe we've got the wrong idea after all.

What aren't we seeing?

Leah went looking for some booze but found the apartment

bizarrely free of whisky. She settled for making herself a cup of tea, and then sat on the sofa, thinking.

"Have you been up all night?"

Leah startled at the sound of Dorian's voice. He walked out into the hallway, heading for the kitchen and the kettle.

She was surprised to see him wearing a holster, complete with gun.

"Iron bullets," said Dorian, when he caught her looking. "Standard issue, Interpol. Unavoidable, although being so close to iron has never sat easy with me. Don't you have them in your time?"

Leah shook her head as Dorian poured the water into a mug. She stared out at the sunrise over Glasgow, bright red, watery, and cold.

"No, but one of the selkies – you know what, never mind."

"Any luck with the case?" asked Dorian, taking a sip of tea.

"Not really," said Leah. "I've been going over what we know. All the folklore I can remember. I've dismissed the idea of a situation where monsters are attacking other monsters, I don't think that's what we've got here. I think it's misdirection."

"Misdirection? You think somebody's trying to send us on a wild goose chase?"

"Someone or something," said Leah. "I keep returning to this monster under the bed idea. Like what Milo said about Fludge, back when he first saw him – all children have one. And what Magnus said about Fludge being dangerous. Kids, monsters, imagination, childlore."

"And your pet, Fludge, is some kind of … infant version of the bogeyman?"

"Either that, or he's full grown. Hard to tell. He's a Spanish folkloric creature, so I don't know much about his species. But all creatures had to start young, I guess. Even you were young once."

"Indeed," Dorian said. "But this wasn't the monster that gave you your scar?"

"No. According to Magnus, that was something else."

"You had more than one monster under your bed? Most children are only issued one."

Leah shrugged.

"Dunno," she said. "Not like I'm trying to hog all the monsters. I have no idea why it would have happened, I'm not privy to monster supply and demand."

"You do find unique ways of getting into trouble, Miss Bishop," he said. "So what happens when he's all grown up?"

"I didn't think of –" Leah began.

Then things fell into place, sudden and fierce, inside her head.

"Holy shit," she said.

CHAPTER TWENTY-ONE

hat is it?" asked Dorian.

Leah gave him a look filled with excitement. She loved it when they finally found the thread and could begin pulling.

"The bogeyman," she said triumphantly.

"The bogeyman?" repeated Dorian. "Leah, that's not just one thing. It's not just Fludge, or Fludge's species. That's *everything*."

"I know," she said. "Folklorist, remember? Cultures all over the world have a bogeyman. Some of those beliefs are held by the entire culture, like *el cucuy*. England's bogeyman is Jenny Greenteeth – well, one of them. Scotland's is *Jenny wi' the airn teeth*, at least for the time being. But each individual child *also* has a bogeyman of their very own. *All children have more than one monster.*"

"The fears of children are powerful," mused Dorian.

"But see, that's just the thing," Leah pursued. "Yeah, a lot of bogeymen punish kids for misbehaving. But there are also bogeymen who protect children and punish the guilty, of any age."

"Regardless of the species, that would not only take an awful lot of power, it would take –"

"Something awfully powerful?" asked Leah. "Or some*one*? Like a demigoddess? The first born in centuries?"

"Like Caoimhe," said Dorian, nodding. "Yes, that makes sense. But Leah, if this is true –"

"*Today, Scotland, tomorrow the world?*" asked Leah. "Yeah, exactly! I know what might be fuelling it in my time, but Dorian – what's fuelling it in yours?"

"Nothing so powerful as Caoimhe, that's for certain," said Dorian.

Leah began to pace again. She glanced out the windows at the sun bleeding red over the rooftops of Glasgow.

"The thing is – I don't think it's Caoimhe herself causing it. She's still far too young."

"So then someone is harnessing her power somehow," said Dorian.

"And probably the same someone has been causing it throughout the years," Leah agreed. "Now, what else has a lot of power that we –"

Her eyes widened.

"Dorian," she said. "Didn't you tell me the reason Interpol is so run-down is because of –"

"Budget cuts," he finished. "We have to talk to Ben."

***

"This is ridiculous," said Leah, as they hurried through the streets toward Interpol. "The man hardly ever leaves the building. How are we going to draw him out?"

"If someone is leaching power from Caledonia, they may be listening to us," said Dorian.

"I wish I had a mobile," grumbled Leah. "I wish you both did, too."

"A mobile?" asked Dorian, puzzled. "Like the toy you put above the bed for children?"

"Well, it's certainly an improvement on open iron scissors hanging above the cradle," Leah said. "But no, that's not –"

Dorian held up a hand as they approached Interpol's exterior.

"Shh," said Dorian. "We don't want the building to get suspicious."

"It gets suspicious?"

"Sure it does. Don't tell me you've never had it conk out on you when you needed to get indoors."

Leah thought of how her palm-print hadn't worked when she'd first arrived.

"Sentient security system?" she asked.

"What do you think all those little giggling lights are?"

"*Those* are the security?"

"Believe me, they pack a punch."

"What are they?"

"Well, the Chief thinks it's more decorative to call them will-o-the-wisps. While that's technically true, it's not entirely accurate."

"Then what are they?"

"Soul-eaters."

Leah went white.

"Oh," she said.

She'd always thought them quaint and cute. A reminder she was entering a magical world.

Suddenly they weren't quite so quaint and cute anymore.

She watched Dorian press his hand to the wall.

To their relief, it glowed around his palm just as it always had, and let them in.

Leah stood at the top of the staircase with its deep ivy canopy. She hesitated.

"Come on then," said Dorian. "Leah, nothing's changed now you know what they are."

"I know," she said, stepping down. "It's just that I always felt safe, past the threshold. Before."

The will o the wisps tittered and giggled in the bushes.

"I always thought they were laughing," she said.

"They are," said Dorian. "It's how they communicate. They're talking about whether we belong here or not."

"Every time?"

"Every time."

"What happens if they decide we don't belong here?"

"Pray that day never comes."

Dorian, for his part, just kept walking. Leah peered into the bushes, trying to catch a glimpse of one of the creatures, when she felt a hand on her elbow.

"Leah," he said, "They don't like to be perceived."

"Oh," she said. "Sorry."

She followed Dorian down the pathway arched with beautiful flowers and climbing ivy. She had always thought it looked like a tropical garden.

She wondered what other kinds of security measures were in

place. If the budget cuts were causing the problem, she wanted all the information available.

"Dorian, what's in the fog beyond the big arched window?" she asked.

"Monsters," he said simply.

"Monsters," she repeated. "Aren't you all monsters?"

"Not like those," said Dorian.

Leah stared at him.

"I take it you didn't read the cryptopedia," commented Dorian. "Or the handbook."

"Cryptopedia?" Leah asked. "I never saw it. And I read the handbook!"

Dorian raised an eyebrow at her.

"Well, *skimmed* might be a better word," she allowed.

"For a researcher, you don't do much research," Dorian observed.

"Hey, I'd just found out monsters were real," Leah retorted. "I had a lot on my plate."

"I wonder what happened to the cryptopedia," said Dorian, as they walked through the door. "Books should not be disappearing like that."

"We only just rediscovered the US Marshals' Grimoire," said Leah.

"What?" asked Dorian, and she realised the magic had prevented him from hearing her again.

"Oh, so I can talk about Caoimhe and Fludge but not the Grimoire?" she asked the open air.

"I take it there's something you're not telling me," said Dorian. "And not on purpose."

Leah nodded.

She stared at the window as they passed by and could just about make out strange shapes in the fog.

"Monsters," she said quietly to herself.

"I can get you a copy of the cryptopedia, if you like."

"Yes, please."

They found themselves in the cavernous Great Hall of Interpol. Leah would never get used to seeing it this way, big and empty, instead of the warm and welcoming place it had been once and would be again.

Dorian went to the wall of books and slid one out.

"On the house," he murmured as he handed it to her.

Ben looked up from his desk as they approached.

"Hiya, Chief," said Leah.

"Good morning, you two," rumbled Ben. "Any news?"

"Yeah!" said Leah brightly. "But we thought you might like to discuss it, you know. Somewhere a little warmer?"

Ben gave them an odd look.

"You certainly are chipper for this time of day," he commented.

"It's a beautiful morning," said Leah, and gave Dorian a desperate look.

"Yes, it's lovely," Dorian rushed to say. "Would you like to join us for a stroll?"

Ben did not look impressed.

"Or a coffee?" Leah cut in. "A nice hot cup of black coffee?"

Ben rubbed his chin.

"Coffee, you say?"

***

"This is momentous," said Ben.

"I know," said Dorian. "The implications of using this kind of power –"

"I meant the coffee," Ben interrupted.

They were seated at a newer café, and Ben was over the moon with the coffee he was drinking.

"I remember when the first coffeehouses were opened in London," said Ben wistfully. "Got a taste for it, and then they opened a café in the Trongate here. That was back in the 1600s. Real coffee craze. Then they shut down everything in favour of pubs. Now it seems to be back in fashion."

"So how does it compare?" asked Leah.

"Favourably," said Ben, as he took a long, appreciative drink. "Now, then. You believe someone is using the power of Interpol to manifest the nightmares of children?"

"Yeah," said Leah. "We thought it safest to tell you out here."

"We don't know who might be listening," Dorian said.

"Good work, detectives," said Ben. "I see why I hired you, Leah."

"Unfortunately, it's only the first half of the puzzle," said Leah. "And I'm unfamiliar with the city during your time period, so I can't be of much help in narrowing down suspects."

"That's all right," said Ben. "We can take it from here."

"And I'm going to have to return to my own time," said Leah. "I was warned not to stay for too long. I think I've found everything worth finding."

CHAPTER TWENTY-TWO

fter Chief Ben left, Dorian and Leah walked from the coffeeshop down to the pub together.

The bar was crowded. Laughter rang out from every direction.

"This is the life," Leah commented, as she drank her whisky and the men around her cheered.

She leaned forward and told Dorian in a conspiratorial whisper:

"You know, I've been thinking about staying –"

"Not for much longer, you're not," said another voice.

Leah froze.

Then she sighed, slumping in her seat.

"Damn it, Aonghas," she said. "You have the *worst* timing."

Aonghas gave her a tired look.

"You're lucky I have any timing at all," he said. "Did you get what you came here to find?"

Leah looked at Dorian, who nodded.

"I think so," she said.

"Then let's get out of here. Daylight's wasting."

"Okay," said Leah, resigned. She set down her glass. "Could you give us a moment?"

"Leah, this is *time-travel,* I'm not sitting outside waiting for you in the car!" Aonghas argued.

"I know, I know," said Leah. "Just – a couple minutes, okay?"

"Fine," said Aonghas. "I'll be right over there when you're ready."

Aonghas walked over to the bar and ordered something Leah couldn't hear.

Dorian stood up when she did.

"I wanted to stay," she told him quietly. "I'd rather stay. Things here, they're...easier."

Dorian gave her a fond smile.

It still seemed such a strange expression on his normally austere face.

"If you mean with me," said Dorian, "just – give me a little time. In any universe, I think we would be best friends. I'm sure that version of me misses you. And I don't think he'd be happy to lose you. I know I'm not. But at least I know, one day, I'll be with you again."

Leah smiled back.

"I wish I knew what made you change," she said. "You seem – I don't know. So much more free."

Dorian shrugged.

"Selkies often have reasons humans might not understand," he said. "Dahlia broke my heart. Sometimes it's easy to forget. Sometimes it isn't. It all depends on the era of our lives."

"Well," said Leah, shaking his hand. "Thank you. For everything."

"Thank *you,* Miss Bishop," said Dorian, drawing her into a hug instead. "You will be missed."

"Will you remember me, do you think?" asked Leah.

"Doubtful," said Dorian. "Time-travel magic has a way of twisting back on itself, putting things right and proper. But we'll remember the clues for the case. However, I'm afraid we may have to wait until your time period to solve it."

"Take care, Dorian Grey," she said, and then nodded to Aonghas, who returned to their table.

"Okay," she told him. "I'm ready."

Aonghas took her by the arm, and she smiled at Dorian one last time.

He tipped his hat to her, and then vanished.

***

"Ouch! Damn it! Watch where you're going!" Leah said, after a hard landing in the present.

Aonghas was shaking his head after slamming into a nearby brick wall.

"Just be grateful we didn't reappear *inside* the wall," groused

Aonghas. "You really cut it close there, Bishop."

"Yeah, yeah," she said, standing up gingerly and brushing herself off. "Thanks for coming to get me."

"Didn't seem like you wanted to leave," Aonghas observed.

"Things were easier there," Leah shrugged. "Everything was different. *Dorian* was different. And maybe –"

"If you had stayed, you could have stopped Magnus?" Aonghas filled in the blanks. Leah nodded.

The Trooping Faerie sighed and crossed his arms.

"Leah, I don't do this very often, so listen up. Okay? There are a lot of people who would use time-travel for those ends," he said. "And I understand. I really do. It's very tempting, to try and go back, to change things. Unfortunately, we found every attempt to better history only resulted in making it worse. Sometimes *much* worse. So when we use time-travel magic now, there are securities put in place to keep it from happening. Staying wouldn't have done you any favours. But we need you here and now, not back then."

"Still doesn't seem fair."

"Never does."

***

Leah walked the streets of Glasgow in the late afternoon light, the strange scent of Tennant's brewery on the cool, damp wind.

She found it refreshing. She found it even *smelled* like home in a way that even the recognisable scent of past-Glasgow did not.

Leah Bishop was a modern Glaswegian. The city was in her bones.

She wandered through Glasgow Green, down past the Barras and the Tolbooth, passing people who were going about their daily business unaware of the existence of monsters, of the return of the Necropolis vampire. People who went to Marks & Spencer and bought their meal specials, including a bottle of wine; people who were already shopping for gifts and planning

179

for Christmas; people who were going to Poundland for the wrapping paper.

And she thought of a selkie in a trenchcoat and a fedora, whose big brown eyes were full of vitality and mischief and *life,* and she wondered what had happened to make him into the Dorian she knew, what had caused him to revert to his stoic Victorian ways.

Although, Leah corrected herself with a smile, it wasn't his Victorian ways that were stoic.

And maybe there was a secret in that, too.

She wondered, not for the first time, if Dorian had been playacting the Victorian stick-in-the-mud all this time later because that was the man Dahlia had wanted, and Dorian considered himself a failure, maybe at fault, for not being a good enough selkie. For not answering the call of seven tears into the sea when he should have; for distracting himself with his own homespun love for Aidan Blake.

The selkie story, she thought, had always been so tragic.

But now they had learned it did not have to be.

It was good for Dorian, and for Robert, to discover they were not trapped within their stories.

For Robert, his own realisation he had not, in fact, been cursed; he was not merely spurred on by terrible magic inflicting him with deep longing for all this time, as everyone had always said. Instead, the love he felt for Desdemona was true. It was freedom, to discover what he felt for Des was a real thing – a creature with a beating heart, just like him.

And for Dorian, to know there was another life available to him, one less tragic and predestined. His past mistakes, his lost loves, all memory.

A future where he might find happiness.

One where he might find love again.

Platonic, or otherwise.

Whether that was in someone's arms, or in the best of friends– well. Leah had her own private hopes.

She found herself in front of the open coffeeshop door of the old subway station, and on impulse went inside and ordered coffee for the three of them. She remembered what Ben had liked the most back in the past and made sure to get him something that resembled it.

For Dorian, she got one of the new sugary specials, because it amused her. She got the same thing for herself.

Then, with all the coffee in a little carrier, she went around the back and placed her hand against the red sandstone.

It glowed around her palm right away, recognising an old friend.

Leah smiled.

She said hello to the will o the wisps as she descended the familiar staircase and walked down the path hanging heavy with ivy and flowers. She opened the studded medieval door that led to Interpol. It closed behind her with a ponderous boom.

Leah waved gaily to the monsters in the mist outside the window as she passed into the Great Hall that served as the central office of Caledonia Interpol.

The fire leapt high in the grate. The brass firedogs played with each other in front of the flames. There were people walking back and forth, in and out of the room, and a few light clouds moved across the ceiling. The walls were piled high with books, and in the distance, she could see Chief Ben working at his desk. The atmosphere was cosy and busy all at once.

Leah's heart was full.

On the sofa in front of the fire, their favourite place to talk over cases, she saw Dorian's familiar silhouette, sitting straight-backed and proper.

She grinned.

Maybe there were some things about the present that were better than the past.

It was good to be home.

CHAPTER TWENTY-THREE

There was something poignant about returning.

Leah stood in the doorway for a moment, caught suspended in a moment of time as she observed Dorian on the couch in front of the fireplace.

She thought about how often she'd thought of him.

Even though she'd been right beside him, in the past, she realised she'd missed her own Dorian far more fiercely than she had known.

Leah thought about endings.

She thought of the last days of summer spent in the warm sunshine among friends. Drinking a cheeky wine hidden in a little bag out in the Botanics as they enjoyed strawberries and cream together, shelved on the gentle slope from which they could survey their surroundings and the other people gathered on the lawns as afternoon stretched to sunset, here at the end of the season.

How those final few summer days were filled with a kind of melancholy, joyful sorrow, and how the things we wish most dearly to grasp to our chests and hold forever have a way of slipping through our fingers like sand.

Appreciate what you've got while you've got it, said a voice inside her, the same voice she trusted when solving the latest mystery, the voice that led her to hunches that usually found their mark. *Because it can be gone, so, so fast – like a summer sunset, like champagne.*

Her university days were behind her now, but how carefree and easy they seemed in retrospect. She felt a bittersweet longing, while understanding now that everything had its time and place.

Leah understood most people felt this way, but most people didn't live the life of Leah Bishop, whose best friend was a supernatural creature and whose job meant stepping in and out of the natural and supernatural worlds.

She was awash in a melancholy feeling of loneliness she couldn't quite pinpoint.

That's pretty damned Scottish of you, she thought to herself with a grin.

Leah knew now that there was something certain here, something that would not fade. She had to do what she could to salvage her friendship with Dorian.

For some people, a romance was the central relationship of their lives.

For both Leah and Dorian, something more akin to platonic true love.

She walked over to the sofa. He stood to greet her, as was his custom, because he was the personification of old-fashioned British politeness.

"Good evening, Miss Bishop," said Dorian. "How was your trip?"

She sat down and he followed suit.

"I missed you," Leah blurted out suddenly, a little startled the words had just *come out* like that.

Dorian looked startled, too.

After a moment's consideration, he spoke.

"I, er, admit I may have felt the same, while in Paris," Dorian confessed. "Leah – there's not much I can do about the man I was in the past, but there is something I can do about the man I choose to be from here onwards. I know it is impertinent to ask, but I'd appreciate a second chance. If you'll be so kind as to be patient with me."

Leah nodded.

"I don't know what's kept Desdemona and Nour best friends for thousands of years," said Leah. "And all I've got is one lifetime."

She swallowed.

"But I'd like to spend it with you."

They smiled at each other.

And in her heart, something eased, something she hadn't even been aware of until that moment.

She thought:
Maybe things are going to get better.

***

They returned to work together, because there wasn't much else to be done while an active case was underway, and they still hadn't solved it.

Leah hoped there would be time, afterward, for more conversations at the pub and shared dinners, the way it had been before their rift.

But they were detectives first and friends second, so it would have to wait.

Leah realised if the Fae didn't need to remain stuck in their stories, then neither did she.

She could decide the way her story would go, and the way that she wanted to live her life.

After all, it wasn't only the Fae who had to deal with societal expectations. Everyone had a story they were expected to follow.

Maybe it was time to choose her own path.

For *everyone* to choose.

CHAPTER TWENTY-FOUR

Their next port of call was to Caoimhe, who they found sitting dejected in the playground at her school.

"What's wrong?" asked Leah.

"My subjects no longer love me," Caoimhe informed her. "They said we were only playing Faerie Queen *last* month. This month, it's pirates."

"We happen to know a real pirate," Dorian told her in a confidential tone. "Her name is Back from the Dead Red."

But Caoimhe was not interested in piracy, and still seemed unhappy.

"Remember what we told you about making friends?" asked Leah gently. "The other children are children *just like you*, Caoimhe."

"But they're *not* just like me!" wailed Caoimhe. "I'm the only one of my kind. Mother said. And the other children –"

She sniffed loudly.

"The other children don't understand, *can't* understand," said Caoimhe, wretched. "I am the first demigoddess in centuries. What else can I be? Mother said we have responsibilities to the humans and –"

"Caoimhe," said Leah. "First, be a little kid. Okay?"

"What would you know about it?" Caoimhe snapped. "You're human, too."

"I know kids can be mean," Leah told her. "A *lot* of kids feel like they don't fit in. And I know what it's like to be the *only* something, because I'm the only human at my job. You may be the only demigoddess, but there are other children who are the *only* something-else, and they feel lonely too. Maybe you could make friends with some of them?"

Caoimhe thought about it.

"I have noticed that a few of them don't seem to be accepted as well as the others," she said slowly. "Some of the children are cruel to them."

"And who better than a demigoddess to be their protector?" asked Dorian. "I'm not human, and I have suffered the judgement of many. But believe me, great friends will come along and guide you, just as well as you have guided them. You would be a wise leader to listen."

He sent Leah a quick smile.

Caoimhe seemed to have perked up at this new idea.

"Perhaps you're right," she said, with a measure of excitement. "I shall befriend these other outsiders and become their guardian! Many great leaders have trained as knights before coming into their own, after all."

Leah and Dorian exchanged a glance, and Leah hid a smile.

"Well, it's something," she allowed.

"By the by," said Caoimhe. "You never did mention whether you had solved the case plaguing my people? The vampire with iron teeth."

"We're still working on it," said Leah. "Are you *sure* it was a vampire with iron teeth you saw, and not something else?"

"I know a monster when I see one, Detective Inspector," said Caoimhe coldly. "As do my subjects, wilful though they may be. I realise we are all of an age, and that is very young, to you and yours. Rest assured, however, we know monsters. As would you, had you seen it."

"Understood."

"Then I thank you, officers, and remain at your disposal."

Then she bowed and swept off across the playground.

"I think that's the end of our audience," said Leah.

"Think she's going to be a great leader?" asked Dorian.

Leah nodded, grinning.

"The best," she said.

***

"I noticed," said Dorian, as they walked along the Clyde together, "that you didn't tell Caoimhe our suspicions."

"That someone might be harnessing her power and driving

these creatures?" asked Leah. "I wasn't sure that was a good idea. She'd probably try to find the perpetrator on her own."

"She has powers beyond mine," said Dorian. "I can cause storms and change the weather. But that is all. Not much use against a formidable foe."

"Even so, it makes me wonder whether she'd even be aware of it," said Leah.

"Or if it's even draining at all," said Dorian. "Caoimhe is unique enough that her power may be greater than we know. These may be questions to ask Aoife instead."

"She's not going to like the idea of her daughter being in danger."

"What else can we do?" asked Leah. "If the power of Interpol was drained before, this has occurred several times over the years. Who knows how long it's been going on, or how long it's going to continue?"

"You know...we may be wrong about Caoimhe," said Dorian. "We have no real evidence in that direction, but the power breaches of Caledonia line up perfectly. That power has lain mostly dormant throughout the years."

"Until someone finds and harnesses it," Leah agreed. "We need to be careful. There are things in the Deeps we wouldn't want to escape."

Dorian nodded, a sour expression on his face.

"Many things," he said, and Leah didn't have to ask.

She knew he was thinking of his brother.

CHAPTER TWENTY-FIVE

eah had been dreading this meeting.

She also knew Dorian couldn't find out about it, which made her feel awful, but there was nothing else she could do.

With a deep sigh of misgiving, she descended the steps into the Deeps.

***

"*Leah,*" said Magnus, in a cadence crawling with smoke.

Had that sinister, snakelike quality always bled through his voice? Or did she only hear it now that it was far too late?

And it *hadn't* been too late, back in the past, but Aonghas's magic, or some other kind of magic, had kept her from speaking.

Apart from one word, *murderer,* which Magnus had heard loud and clear –

probably because it had included a reference to his own past, even though it turned out he hadn't been the perpetrator.

At least, not that time.

"Magnus," Leah greeted him coldly. "I'm here for information, nothing more."

Magnus gave her a searching look, his big brown eyes so wide and welcoming, so innocent, she'd be tempted if she didn't know better.

"Where's Dorian?" he sniffed the air. "All I smell here is human."

"Dorian's not coming," said Leah.

"What a shame," said Magnus, as if it really wasn't. He smiled, slowly and far too wide. "I do so like our little family reunions. I take it he doesn't even know you're here."

"No. He doesn't."

"So what can I do for you, Leah, down here with the monsters all alone?" he asked with a smirk, as if this was a victory.

Something about what he'd said arrowed through her. She realised Magnus was the least of her worries. She really had no idea exactly *what* had been imprisoned down here throughout the millennia. The weakening of the Interpol defences might release unspeakable creatures out into the living world of Glasgow once again.

If the magic of the Deeps had been compromised, that meant Leah was treading on thin ice here, a small and human creature in the jaws of a great slavering beast.

We police our own, Dorian and Ben had often said. *The ones who need policing.*

Not all monsters are reformed.

We are all one drink shy of falling off the wagon, Milo had told them once, in an almost-forgotten, long-ago conversation.

Leah was in danger, and she knew it, although she did not yet know what form it would take.

She decided to depend upon Magnus's affection for her, as opposed to the alternatives –

better the Devil you know,

Magnus the beautiful, the Lucifer of Caledonia.

"Tell me, Detective," purred Magnus. "How can I help you?"

Leah steeled herself and focused on the task at hand.

"We believe these monsters have been created by someone harnessing the power of Caledonia," she said. "First we knew about it was back in the 50s, then the 70s."

"And now," said Magnus.

"It's also possible that whoever is doing it today is harnessing Caoimhe's power somehow."

"Aoife's daughter?" asked Magnus, puzzled. "Why?"

"You tell me."

"I confess, Detective Bishop, on this one you've got me stumped."

"The problem is that this draining of power is weakening Interpol. Especially its defences. Perhaps you've noticed."

"I admit I have seen a few things that were cause for concern down here, yes."

"What do you remember, of the time I travelled to the past?"

Magnus blinked, clearly not expecting the abrupt change of subject. He shrugged lightly.

"Not much," he said. "Time travel has a tendency to work itself out, you see. Too many paradoxes. Too many secrets. That sort of thing."

"Well, I'll tell you what *I* remember," said Leah, her voice a little stronger now.

Magnus actually took a step back.

This surprised Leah. He had always been so self-assured.

But she pressed on.

"I remember a selkie as lonely and lost as Dorian," said Leah. "Flashy parties, all the money in the world, nicest flat in the city, and not even your *maid* gave a shit whether you lived or died. But you know who did?"

Magnus stared at her for a moment, holding her gaze.

"I –" he said, then his eyes flicked downward in a gesture of submission. "Dorian. Of course."

"Loneliness can do awful, terrible things to a person," said Leah, approaching the door. "Like maybe – someone with an in as to how Interpol works, someone with a crowbar to jimmy things open a little bit, *someone who would do anything to be free.*"

Leah gave him a hard stare.

"If you're doing this, Magnus, you need to come clean," Leah said. "You can't do this to Dorian. Don't break his heart. Not again."

Magnus looked up at her.

"Leah, you think –" he began, and the snake-soft sound had vanished from his voice, leaving only a naked fear. "You said something is stealing the power from Caledonia, maybe from Caoimhe. How could you think I'm doing it?"

"You have the motive. And the knowledge. *And* the longevity."

"But not the wherewithal. As to who was doing it before,

I can't answer that," said Magnus. "But I know for certain it wasn't me, and I'm not the one doing it now. Leah, I'm..."

He swallowed visibly, his gaze wandering to focus on something behind her.

She glanced over her shoulder but saw nothing.

"To be perfectly honest with you, I'm terrified," said Magnus, as she turned back to face him. "And late at night, I hear the others – they're afraid, too."

Leah was taken aback.

"What kind of monster do other monsters fear?" she asked.

"We are not the oldest monsters," said Magnus in a soft voice. "Some of them have been here for thousands of years. Anything even resembling humanity is long gone. If they get out, the rest of us can count our remaining days on one hand. Leah – we're *all* in danger. *You're* in danger, most of all."

Suddenly, he made a panicked, aborted move toward the door as if to open it, staring at something she could not see.

His eyes were huge and bulging. He spoke in an urgent undertone.

"I thought this might happen," he said. "Leah, I *know* you don't trust me, and you have absolutely no reason to listen to me, but I am *begging* you, open this door."

"And let you out?" scoffed Leah.

"No, to let you *in*," said Magnus in a rush. "Please. You invoked my brother's name, and the one thing he will *never* forgive me is if I let you die on my watch! Get in here! Now!"

Leah rolled her eyes and opened her mouth to reply.

That was when she heard the sound.

The sarcastic retort died on her lips.

That whispering noise, like some great insect was crawling up the stairs.

The same insect sounds she had heard in Morrison's.

On her beetle feet.

"*Leah, please!*" Magnus burst out in agony, thumping his fist against the door of his cell.

Leah glanced behind herself and finally saw the great shadow of the creature on the wall, human-headed, cockroach-bodied; and she made a split-second decision.

She placed her hand against the door, and it glowed as she wrenched it open.

The creature on the stairwell screamed and charged.

Leah and Magnus threw their weight against the door and it slammed shut, locking tight, just as the creature collided with it, shrieking in anger.

It threw itself against the door as they leaned against it together, feeling every bone-shaking moment of impact.

Leah looked over at Magnus in the gloom.

In the low shadows of the cell, as the monster kept up its attack, the selkie smiled at her.

In an instant, she came face to face with the reality that she was now locked inside a cell in the Deeps of Caledonia Interpol with Magnus Grey.

eah stared at Magnus in the gloom as the monster shrieked its impotent fury against the door.

"Don't worry," he whispered. "I meant what I said, Leah, about Dorian. I would never."

"Guess it's too bad none of those other women were as important to your brother as I am," snarled Leah.

"You chose to come in here."

"Like I had a choice!"

The door was near-rattling off its hinges when the noise abruptly stopped.

Leah looked up at the door and her gaze snapped to Magnus. This time, she could *see* him shine.

Leah felt the rise of the selkie-magic, but as one feels the warmth of a nearby flame, because it wasn't directed at her.

Magnus's eyes were closed, and he was beautiful; lovely almost beyond human comprehension, as light suffused his being.

Eventually, the monster outside shuffled away.

As the whispering footsteps receded, Magnus opened his eyes, bright with the blue of the sea, until they faded back to the usual rich dark brown of the seal-men.

"I thought, if the defences of the Deeps are down, I could use my own magic to, er, *politely suggest* there was nothing here of real interest."

"Great," she told him. "Thanks. Now what?"

"I take it you don't have mobile coverage down here."

Leah took her phone out of her pocket and looked at it.

"Zero bars," she confirmed. "Magic or not, mobiles still don't work in basements."

"Look, Leah," Magnus began, but she held a hand up.

"We're not starting," she said. "We're not doing anything, okay?"

Magnus sighed and ran a hand through his beautiful hair.

"Suit yourself," he said. "And I understand why you feel that way, I do. I've had a long time to think down here. I'm not asking for forgiveness or anything. I know better. But since we have no idea how long it's going to take before somebody comes down here and finds us, you may as well fill me in. I could be of assistance."

Leah sighed angrily and went to sit down on the bench with a thump.

"Fine," she said. "It's a way to pass the time, I guess."

And she told him every single detail she could remember.

***

An hour later, Magnus was staring up at the ceiling, thinking.

"Any ideas?" pressed Leah. "Like when they're going to come round to give you food and let me out of here?"

Magnus turned to her suddenly.

"Loneliness," he said. "Something with which I am intimately familiar, as you well know. You made reference to it yourself."

"Loneliness?" repeated Leah. "What the hell do you mean?"

"Well," said Magnus. "People will do just about anything when they're lonely. Selkies – we're *supposed* to have partners, we're *meant* for it, *built* for it."

"This is your motive?" Leah asked disdainfully.

"When you say it that way, I know you mean *this is your excuse?*" Magnus said. "And the answer to that question is both yes and no. All I can tell you is that monsters are monsters because they do something outside the bounds of society, and unlike humans, monsters tend to go strange if they are not able to live out their purpose."

"Well, the only monster I know whose reputation for loneliness precedes them is urisks," said Leah. "And Yoo Min murdered Gregoire. Not that I approve of extrajudicial murder in any case but his actions –"

"Punishment fits the crime," said Magnus with a nod. "Don't look at me that way, Leah. I'm agreeing with you. Although in this particular case, I don't mean *one* monster."

"What?"

"I mean *all of them,*" said Magnus. "The Deeps has been here since, well. Long before I ever even knew of Interpol's existence."

"And you're suggesting...what?"

"You caught the edges of it when you accused me. I assume you're familiar with *The Count of Monte Cristo.*"

Leah started.

"A prison break."

"Yes."

"What monster would do that?"

Magnus smiled again, sardonic and sad.

"Oh, Leah," he said. "What monster wouldn't?"

CHAPTER TWENTY-SEVEN

ow long before Yoo Min comes down for dinner?"

"Depends. She keeps her own schedule."

"What's that like?"

"Having my liver ripped out and eaten daily? It's an experience."

"Well *I* have to eat, and drink, even if you don't."

"I do. Sometimes they give me fish in ice. They say it's enrichment."

"Fascinating."

Magnus stared up at the ceiling again, his eyes fixed there as if he saw the answers to the universe printed in the paint.

"Don't worry, Leah. There's no need to wait for her."

"How do you figure?"

Here, even now, he was beautiful, in the play of light and shadow on the wall.

"I cannot be redeemed," he said. "I know that now. But I can make a start."

"What do you mean?"

He looked at her, the low light starting in his eyes.

"If the defences of the Deeps are weak, then I can open this door."

"If *you* can open the door, so can the other monsters. They could be waiting out there."

"I'm counting on it."

"Magnus –"

"You know, the selk," said Magnus, thinking aloud, "have the law of attraction on our side. I can draw them toward me, and away from you. Although you'll need to resist the selkie-charm – but that shouldn't be hard, since you've had plenty of practise, and you're not bound by story like the rest of us."

"How is that going to work?"

"You remember the stories of the Dionysian women?"

"They went mad and tore the men limb from – *oh*."

She stared at him, shaking her head, ready to protest.

The selkie held up a hand.

"Leah. I've had much time to think, and to dwell on my crimes. Let me do this one thing. It may not be redemption, but it's something. For you. For Dorian, who I've disappointed for so long, and in so many ways."

Leah stared at him. She had deep misgivings about this plan, since it could be just one more of Magnus's tricks.

But she also wanted the door open. She could deal with the consequences later. Besides, if he was right, they were all in danger.

"When we get outside this door, I want you to run up the stairs as fast as you can," Magnus told her. "You'll have about a minute, two minutes tops. Get behind the upper door and bar it behind you. Whatever is affecting the magic down here can't reach the exterior walls. The Deeps have a magic all their own."

Leah swallowed, and gave a sharp nod, not trusting herself to speak.

Magnus turned, and she could feel the lilt and lift of the selkie cantrip; that undeniable, unavoidable attraction rising like a wave.

There was a loud *thunk,* and the door swung open.

They walked out into the hallway, cautious and on their guard.

"Maybe –" Leah began, when she heard the sound.

Something was rushing up the stairs towards them. It was coming on fast.

"Go," Magnus said.

Leah could feel the intensity of that seductive attraction like a pressure on her skin.

She hesitated, and Magnus shoved her toward the stairs.

"*Go!*" he shouted, and she broke into a run, throwing herself onto the staircase and taking them two at a time.

There was a terrible sound, of creaking doors and footsteps and a hushed susurrus of activity coming closer, approaching like a storm.

Leah paused and looked down.

The hallway beneath her spread out with darkness like a shadow filled and coloured in; Magnus's face, bright and beatific, shining, a man treading water just before he is pulled under the waves for good.

"Goodbye, Leah," called Magnus. "Tell my brother I love him."

He disappeared, then, beneath the roiling black.

Leah turned and ran.

She burst through the door and spun around, slamming it shut. Then she slid the bolt home.

Leah sprinted off toward the Great Hall where she all but collided with Dorian.

"Leah!" Dorian's panicked voice echoed in the vastness of Caledonia's entrance hallway as she nearly barrelled right into him.

He caught her and held her by the elbows as he demanded:

"Where have you *been,* we've been searching *everywhere –*"

"I was in the Deeps," she said, breathless, hating the look of horror etched across his face. "The defences are down, we were right. I trapped them behind the door, but –"

"Them?"

"The monsters."

She caught her breath, and put a hand on his shoulder, steadying herself against him.

"Jenny found me," she said. "And I went into Magnus's cell, to get away from her."

Dorian's already-pale face turned even whiter.

"Are you all right?"

Leah nodded.

"Yes," she told him. "But Dorian. I need to tell you something."

"What? What is it?"

"It's Magnus. He's – your brother is dead. I'm so sorry."

***

The fire crackled softly in the fireplace.

The brass firedogs sat alert. They seemed to sense the sombreness of the moment, and so were not their usual playful selves, but watched Dorian from their posts beneath the flames.

"Magnus was a monster," was all he had said, cold and British, in response to the news. "But he was also my brother."

Then he'd sat down on the long sofa and buried his face in his pale white hands.

Dorian's tears streamed freely, although he did not make a sound.

Leah sat with him, just as quiet, her hand on his back, as she watched the firedogs observe them both with canine concern.

CHAPTER TWENTY-EIGHT

"I'm sorry to bring this up, but we still have a problem."

Leah looked at Chief Ben, who was standing a respectful distance away.

"Yeah, okay," said Leah, standing up.

She laid a hand on Dorian's shoulder.

"I'll be all right alone here, Miss Bishop," he said tightly. "Do not worry yourself unduly. In fact, I might favour a bit of time on my own."

Leah nodded.

"Text me if you need anything," she said.

Then she turned to Ben.

"What are you thinking?"

He walked out into the corridor and indicated the door to the Deeps.

It was bending outward, creaking like a door in a horror film.

It almost looked like it was breathing.

Leah looked at it askance.

"We safe out here, Chief?" she asked, as she joined him near the window.

In the murky darkness of the mist beyond the glass, she thought she saw something move.

"Well, I haven't always been here, surprising as that may seem," he explained. "So I have no idea if there is anything we can do about the situation."

"There must be a failsafe of some kind," Leah reasoned. "Nobody would build a maximum-security prison like this one – even a magical prison – and then leave it unguarded. They must have known this might be a possibility someday."

"I would have thought the same," Ben told her. "But I was never made aware of anything. Perhaps there is an alarm system. Or something –"

They were interrupted by a loud creak.

And then a crack.

"Should we –" Leah began.

The door splintered and burst open.

"Ah, shit," sighed Leah, in a resigned voice.

"Run!"

Leah had never seen Ben move so fast.

She looked over her shoulder.

Creatures were pouring into the hallway, flooding past the broken door.

Suddenly, the glass of the great window exploded outward. It shattered as the shards fell to the ground and littered the floor in front of Ben and Leah as they shielded themselves from the debris.

Then Leah looked up.

Enormous, black, slimy tentacles burst through the broken window out of the endless fog, snatching up every creature that was pouring through of the doorway and dragging them over the precipice.

What followed were the most horrific tearing, rending, *eating* sounds Leah had ever heard, emanating from the mist beyond the window.

Then the tentacles withdrew back into the dark fog of the mysterious courtyard beyond.

Within moments, it was over.

Leah and Ben cautiously got to their feet.

The heavy wooden door to the Deeps had been completely destroyed, hanging in pieces from its frame.

The hallway beyond, leading to the prison below, was empty. There was no further sound or movement.

The Deeps, Leah figured, were now empty, too.

"So that's the security system," said Ben faintly.

After a moment, he continued.

"I suppose I'll have to get the window repaired."

"And the door," said Leah.

"Indeed."

***

Glasgow seemed even greyer after Magnus's passing.

Quite a feat, for such a grey city.

There had always been such a stern austerity to the place, its ancient coal-marked buildings cut with those washed sandstone-red.

But there was a beauty in it, all the same.

Now, for them, it had lost some of its lustre.

Things had changed.

Leah wandered alone along her favourite pathways, Kelvin Bridge and the Kelvin Walk, emerging onto the university grounds in the darkness.

Everyone is loved by someone.

Even the worst of us, she thought.

The world was a strange place.

Some monsters could die of old age, it was true, but that was very, very old, and few could be killed outright.

That was the curse of true immortality.

Selkies were one such creature.

This made Magnus's demise all the more terrible –

as a creature who could not die by normal means, he would have been fully aware as he was taken apart.

Whether such a fate could end the long life of a seal-man for good, Leah did not know.

Neither, she suspected, did Dorian, and so it was a particular type of grief not felt by many walking the earth.

It was the thing that had driven Gregoire mad during the Fae Wars, the idea that there was suffering without end.

Death, he had told her once, *was a blessing only meant for mortal souls.*

***

When Leah finally made her way back to Interpol, she found Dorian waiting for her.

"Are you sure you're ready –"

"Leah, please," said Dorian, and she could tell he was distraught by the tone of his voice. "I need to work. Get my mind off things."

"Okay," she said gently. "You want to get out of here for a while?"

"Yes, absolutely."

They went upstairs to the coffeeshop that crowned Interpol.

Leah had always been somewhat amused by the fact that although Caledonia was an ancient police station, the people at the coffeeshop itself were none the wiser. They had no idea about the expansive world beneath their feet, composed of Scotland's history, culture, and folklore from time out of mind.

"You know," Leah said, as she sipped her black coffee and Dorian enjoyed his sugary concoction, "I've been thinking a lot about my own childhood, what with the case and all."

"Indeed," said Dorian vaguely, clearly away with the faeries.

"You never did tell me why you like that stuff so much," said Leah, indicating his drink.

Dorian shrugged.

"Coffee was all the rage in London when I was younger, just as Ben said," he told her. "Sugar was an extreme luxury. The combination of both seems wildly extravagant."

He took a sip.

"Besides, it's delicious," he said. "I assure you there is no need to assert your *toughness* by drinking the bitterest brew, or the harshest whisky."

"Well, that stings," said Leah, laughing.

"You ought to know the truth of it."

"I guess so," said Leah. "Anyway. I was thinking – of my mum. I lost her, years ago, in a car accident. Dad was never the same after that, and he passed away a few years later. Something they say, you can die of a broken heart."

"That is true. Humans can, at the very least," said Dorian, a little mournful.

"But I was thinking of Mum," said Leah, "and how, when you're little, everything your parents tell you to do seems like a big ask, like it's impossibly unfair. But then you grow up, and you find out there was a reason they told you not to put your hand on the hob."

"Selkies have a different sort of upbringing," Dorian offered. "But I take your point. However, what can we glean from that, for the case?"

"I'm thinking we've been making a mistake, all this time, trying to find out information from the very young," said Leah.

"By which you mean we should be questioning the very old? We did speak with Beira."

"Yeah, but there's old and there's old," said Leah. "And then, there's old and *Glaswegian*."

"Someone who would have been here for any and all instances of the Gorbals Vampire."

"Exactly."

"I think I know someone."

CHAPTER TWENTY-NINE

"I'm not the oldest Glaswegian."

Leah and Dorian stared in surprise at Desdemona, whose red curls fell over bare white shoulders as she wrapped a veil around her dance costume and walked with them to the back of her club. Smoke seemed to follow her, emanate from her; sometimes Leah suspected she was made of smoke, and only solidified when someone was looking directly at her.

Desdemona lit a cigarette and blew the smoke out between bright candied-cherry red lips.

Her green eyes had a fire all their own, reflecting the glow of her cigarette.

"If not you," asked Dorian, "then who?"

Desdemona smirked.

"Thought you two were detectives," she said.

Then she sighed.

"Look, didn't Robert tell you anything?" she asked Leah.

"Plenty," said Leah, "too much, at times. He's so *sad.*"

"Tell me about it," said the *baobhan sith*, taking another drag. "Well, if he didn't communicate the information: the one you're looking for is Nour."

"I didn't think you were much younger."

"I'm not," said Desdemona. "A few days, maybe. But it's not my own antiquity you're looking for – it's time in Glasgow. And Nour is definitely that person. She's the oldest Glaswegian by either measure: time alive, or time spent here."

She crushed her cigarette in the ashtray.

"But you're going to have your work cut out for you."

"What do you mean?" asked Leah.

"Well, she isn't exactly a friend to straight answers," said Desdemona. "Unlike some of us, who are a little more direct."

There, behind her eyes, Leah saw the eldritch horror that Desdemona *really* was, just for an instant – and recoiled.

This seemed to amuse her, because Desdemona laughed.

"When Robert saw that for the first time – the *real me*, such as I am, for the first time, it only brought him closer," said Desdemona. "Man in love with death, if you ask me."

"Man in love with monsters," said Dorian smoothly. "Those do exist in this world, at least."

The music kicked on again, slow and earthy.

"As scintillating as this conversation has been, detectives," said Desdemona, "I'm on. All my best to you – and I do hope you catch this so-called vampire."

She grinned.

A little *too* impossibly wide, with a few too many teeth.

It was unsettling.

"This is *my* territory, after all."

And she turned away, looking for all the world like a normal human woman. Desdemona went out into the crowd in a swirl of smoke and beads and silk. The visceral beat of the music filled the club, dark, exotic, and dangerous.

"Well, that's more than we usually get," said Dorian. "She must be in a good mood tonight."

***

Nour, as it turned out, was not so easy to find.

She didn't seem to have a regular haunt or place of abode.

When they finally found her, she was contemplating some of the more interesting stock in the Museum of Anatomy in the Hunterian at Glasgow University.

"I have a ticket. Made a reservation and everything, officers," said Nour, proudly waving it at them.

"That's great, Nour. We've been looking for you. Don't you have a house or flat?"

Nour gave them a puzzled look.

"I'm a bird, silly," she said. "Later I thought I'd perch over the quad and drop fifty-pound notes on the students."

"That's very generous of you."

"The view is excellent from there. I have heard of humans giving 'tips' and would like to try it."

"Okay," said Leah.

"I'm also considering doing something illegal later," said Nour, "if you'd like to join."

"We're police officers," said Dorian.

"Oh, nothing *too* illegal, you understand," Nour rushed to say. "Just to find out what it's like."

"Nour," said Leah, "Desdemona tells us you're the oldest Glaswegian."

"Been here the longest!" she chirped. "Oldest, I can't say. A few others, maybe Aonghas."

"We're investigating sightings of the vampire with iron teeth," said Dorian. "So far our leads haven't led anywhere."

"Hmm," said Nour. "You know. If I didn't have Desdemona. Well. You know. I don't know."

"What?" asked Leah.

"Old age is a lonely place," said Nour. "Immortals are ageless. Now, may I go?"

Dorian sighed.

"Yes, of course," said Dorian.

Nour smiled brightly and swept out of the room.

"Cryptic as usual," said Leah.

"Maybe not so much this time."

"Oh?" she asked. "You got something out of that?"

"Immortals with mortal friends tend to lose them," Dorian said. "I think that's what she meant about Desdemona. They've remained together all this time and so loneliness has never really bitten either of them."

Leah turned this information over in her mind.

"So," she said, "if old age is lonely…immortal old age is lonelier still."

Leah walked in companionable silence with Dorian along the banks of the Clyde on their way back to Interpol.

The sun was setting in a distant sky, pink and orange through the low clouds that tended to hang above the city.

"We have had many adventures together," said Dorian abruptly, bringing Leah out of her thoughts. "I am a fortunate seal to have found a friend like you, Leah."

Leah smiled at him.

"Me too," she said. "Fortunate human, anyway. I'm sorry about your brother, Dorian."

The selkie nodded.

"As am I," he said. "But I am glad, in the end, he went well. I often wonder what suffering will do. For some, it strengthens them. And for some, it makes them cause suffering themselves. There is no excuse. One who has suffered ought to know better. But I console myself that he did the right thing at the very end."

"Which still leaves us with nothing to go on and nowhere to go as far as the case is concerned," Leah said. "Although..."

She stuck her hands in her pockets and stared out across the flat plane of the Clyde reflecting the cranes and bridges of the city.

"Although?" repeated Dorian.

"As a child," Leah said slowly, "you and Magnus faced a human man, a seal-hunter."

"Yes."

"One that had no experience of selkies."

"Well, it's not that odd. Most people have forgotten us over the years. Scotland is not as it once was with regards to story-telling."

"So what happens when folklore is forgotten, and the children no longer remember?"

CHAPTER THIRTY

"Childlore is dangerous now?"

"Only the lore that has been forgotten. What happens to any of you when the stories change?"

"We change. You've seen Aonghas."

"Right. And if the stories are forgotten?"

Dorian stared at her and gripped the handle of his walking stick.

"We cease to be."

"And what monster wouldn't go out of its way to ensure its existence? Like Magnus said. What monster wouldn't go out of its way to ensure its freedom?"

"Or what human, come to that."

"Or even –"

Leah smacked Dorian on the arm.

"Miss Bishop!" he scolded her.

She turned a look full of fire on him.

"A goddess," she said. "Come on, Dorian. I think we need to pay a visit to an old lady."

***

Beira was whistling as she busied herself pouring tea.

Leah rapped on the door.

"Come in, my darlings," she said. "I've been expecting you."

Old Man Snorfles greeted them at the door with a wag of his tail and looked up at them with cloudy eyes.

Leah gave him an absentminded pat on the head, and after receiving this tribute, he waddled off to curl up by the fire.

"One *does* need to do something dramatic to be noticed these days," Beira sighed as she sat down and arranged all her blankets around herself. Most were browns and tans – the colours of autumn, with a few white ones here and there: a sign of the imminent change in seasons. "Youth, as they say, is wasted on the young."

"We will have to arrest you. Where are the children, Beira?" asked Dorian.

"Will you indeed? The children are fine. Playing with the wee ones of our kind, you know. Fairy reels, all that."

"Last I checked, those who danced the fairy reels ended up outside of their own time," Leah said.

"Not much can be done about that. Besides, they weren't *real* children. Not really. Blame the sensationalist tabloid press."

"Not real children? What the hell does that mean?"

"She means that she changed adults into children, like she did with us," said Dorian. "I thought you above the wicked witch antics, Beira. How uncouth."

"Uncouth? My laddie. These people. They are so unhappy. Life has been hard on them, to say the very least. Now they are children again. They dance with our own children, happy and carefree."

"Their families are missing them," said Leah.

"I wish the world could be as it was," said Beira. "I bring the winter. Cleansing. The cold and the snow. And yet I am forgotten in favour of the young and handsome."

She gestured toward Dorian.

"I am hardly young," he said.

"When counted in years, perhaps, but I came into existence as an old woman. An old woman I remain. Once upon a time, that garnered respect. Faith. Not so nowadays. And you see how these people today treat their elderly. Disposable, expendable. Forgotten. Things were not so in the past.

"Today, people care more for monsters. So I thought, here is a way to ensure I won't be forgotten."

"How did you go from being the Old Woman of Winter to the vampire with iron teeth?" asked Leah.

"Because there never was such a thing," said Beira. "There is no vampire with iron teeth. There never has been, which is why you were having such a hard time finding it.

"Just as tradition can be invented, so too can folklore. New stories.

"The vampire with iron teeth was entirely an invention. These stories are like empty vessels, looking for something to fill and embody them. Some never find their purpose and are like story-ghosts. Others find those gods and monsters who are beginning to be lost to time, and so they become one with that legend in order to ensure their survival."

"There was a prison break at the Deeps. It resulted in the deaths of many monsters, including Dorian's brother."

"I am sorry to hear that. But I am not the cause. Just an opportunist. I took the power leaching out of Interpol, but the budget cuts are the real culprit."

Beira picked up her knitting.

"I did not take the power of that young one, as you seemed to believe. She will come into her own with it soon enough. But no, Interpol has always been enough for me. Call it survival – anytime the defences were weakened, I saw my chance. I never thought much of it, since it seemed an honest trade. Those children returned to their youth for a while and were able to enjoy some measure of happiness. Don't you worry – when the story fades again, they revert to their adult selves, a little well-rested and happier for it, just as you did. There's a reason the tales of the vampire with iron teeth never turned up victims. They didn't exist."

"Why didn't you just *tell* us?"

"Where's the faith in that? I do not ask for fame, Dorian. Only survival. Without the story, I would not survive. So I couldn't tell you. The story had to be told."

Dorian sighed in frustration.

"Leah. A word."

They ducked outside together, into a light, misty rain.

"Budget cuts at Caledonia Interpol also meant cuts in security," said Leah. "We thought someone was harnessing Caoimhe's power, but it turns out the timing was just coincidence."

"Every one of these appearances of the vampire with the iron teeth coincides with the budget cuts at Caledonia Interpol."

"Leaving it open to attack. Like with hackers," said Leah. "And one of the Guardians vanished once. Now two are gone."

"Who *exactly* is cutting the budget, anyway?" asked Dorian. "Are we a government office? Does the *government* cut the budget, or is it somebody else? *Where is Ben sending his paperwork?*"

"Those are all good questions, and things we should investigate when we have the time. But what do you want to do right now?"

Dorian stared out at the rain for a while.

"I am uncomfortable with arresting her," he said.

"Me too," said Leah. "What harm's been done, after all? If the prison break wasn't her fault, and she returns everyone intact."

"But she did break the law."

"Dorian. I know you want there to be justice for what happened to Magnus, but sometimes things happen for reasons of negligence, or because that's just the way of the world."

"Such as it is, yes. Our laws are somewhat more fluid than your own. But I take your meaning."

"What do we tell Ben?"

"The truth. I'd see if he wants to prosecute, but somehow, I doubt it. I think he will be of the same mind, in the end."

Leah glanced through the window into the warm living room and did not see a criminal.

She saw a lonely old woman offering her dog a biscuit.

One who would look forward to visits from family and grandchildren, only Beira had none.

So she was alone.

And in a flash, Leah saw her own possible future.

Loneliness, and what it can do.

Not that she would ever go to such extreme lengths, but she was human, and didn't need people to remember her story in order for her to survive.

"Agreed," Leah relented, and Dorian gave a sharp nod of acknowledgement.

Back inside, Dorian laid out their proposal to Beira.

"If you agree to release all the people you have captured, we will not arrest you," said Dorian. "But we will be keeping a close eye on you for the rest of your days. You cannot do this again, Beira. Is that understood?"

Beira nodded.

"You are a good seal, Dorian," she said. "Better than I would be, I should think, were I a seal myself. Now that the legend is circulating again, my survival is no longer of concern. For the time being, at least."

"Wouldn't you rather be remembered as Beira – who you *really* are, the Old Woman of Winter – instead of a shell you inhabited like a hermit crab?" asked Leah.

Beira shrugged.

"It matters very little to me, as long as I survive."

***

The return of the missing people to their families was a joyful one, and was marked as one of Caledonia Interpol's greatest successes.

As for Beira, her home in Bridgeton was locked up for the winter.

She had gone home.

The great mountain of Cruachan in Dalmally was white with Beira's plaid.

The power station came to life beneath the silent stone.

The glen was often dark and cold, since the sun only made a brief appearance before it was obscured by the mountains.

The wind shaped the snowdrifts and blessed the ground.

A giant of a man stood at the foot of Ben Cruachan, a lone figure laying a rose against the brilliant white.

"You are not forgotten," said Chief Ben, and he turned to leave.

In the slate-grey sky above him, it began to snow.

eah watched Ben from the sofa.

She had never seen him wear a suit before.

He took the slender, long-stemmed rose that Robert had given him from its vase with a secret smile.

"Chief," she ventured. "Do you have a date?"

Ben blushed.

Leah's jaw dropped.

"You *do*," she gasped.

"Please, Miss Bishop. Could we keep this quiet for the time being?"

Leah grinned.

"Whatever you say," she told him. "But you gotta know the secretaries will be gossiping about it, at least."

"Pardon me, I don't mean to interrupt."

Leah's jaw dropped. She knew that voice.

She turned to see Beira standing there with Old Man Snorfles at her feet.

"Good evening, Leah. Shall we, Benandonner?" she asked, hooking her arm toward him. "We have reservations at Two Fat Ladies for seven o'clock."

"Before we go, I'd like you to meet someone," said Ben.

Aoife emerged with Caoimhe beside her, holding her hand.

"I know a little girl who might need a grandmother. Caoimhe?"

Caoimhe hid behind Aoife's legs, the first time Leah had ever seen her bashful.

"Caoimhe, this is Beira," said Ben.

"Pleased to make your acquaintance," said Beira.

Caoimhe just stared up at her.

"I'm a goddess," Beira told Caoimhe. "Would you like to learn from me?"

"Yes, ma'am," said Caoimhe.

Beira offered her hand, and Caoimhe solemnly shook it.

"No one is forgotten if they become family," said Ben.

Leah watched the entire exchange. It was a revelation.

"Detective Inspector," Ben said suddenly. "Don't you have some work you should be getting on with?"

"Sure thing, Chief," said Leah, turning to busy herself with the paperwork.

"And Detective?" he reminded Leah under his breath, as he offered Beira the slightly crushed rose. "Not a word."

Leah made the sign of zipping her lips as she grinned at him, and she watched him go.

"Guess Chief finally got that Valentine after all," she thought to herself.

The following day, word had spread through Caledonia Interpol like wildfire.

But Leah hadn't said a thing.

***

"Leah."

Leah looked up and Dorian nodded toward the corridor.

Standing at the other end of the hall, in the empty space between the broken door to the Deeps and the broken window, was a monster.

Jenny wi' the airn teeth.

"Why didn't she get grabbed by the monsters?" Leah whispered.

Dorian regarded the creature with some interest.

"There must be a reason," he whispered back. "Perhaps we were too quick to judge."

Then Jenny noticed them.

She saw they were looking at her, and she clasped her claws together.

Almost as if she were…shy.

"Leah, how did you know that song?" Dorian asked under his breath. "You recognised it. I thought at first it was just because you were a folklorist, but did your parents sing it to you when you were a child?"

"Are you trying to say I manifested the vampire with the iron teeth?" Leah demanded.

"Not on purpose, but –"

Jenny screamed, softly this time.

She seemed to hesitate before moving forward.

"You may approach," said Dorian, his eyes lighting blue as the selkie cantrip was invoked, mostly out of protection for Leah than anything else.

She screamed again, even more quietly.

Dorian paused.

"She's *speaking*," said Dorian. "Those screams are *words*, Leah."

"You couldn't have figured that out at Morrison's?"

"I couldn't hear it before, not without the selkie magic. In human form, it just sounds as it does to you – like screaming."

Jenny stood before them now, tall and horrifying.

Leah did her best to hold her ground.

Then, Jenny reached out a clawed hand and touched the scar on Leah's cheek.

"She says she cannot express how sorry she is that this happened," Dorian translated the mournful hoots issuing from Jenny's mouth. "She only wanted to protect you. She has never eaten children, she says – she doesn't have the taste for them. A cruel rumour, apparently."

"It was you," said Leah, in belated recognition. "You protected me."

Jenny nodded.

Leah reached out and took her hand.

"And you were trying to protect me again."

Jenny nodded again.

"People distrust the things they fear and don't understand," said Leah, looking into Jenny's sad expression. "I'm so sorry, Jenny."

But Jenny smiled. Leah's kindness was thanks enough.

"Looks are deceiving," murmured Dorian.

"Agreed," said Leah, thinking of Magnus Grey.

"She'd like to know if she can stay."

***

As it turned out, Jenny was very sweet, and enjoyed baking.

She and Beira took it upon themselves to be Caoimhe's guides and babysitters, leaving a very thankful Aoife free to work at Interpol in her usual guise as receptionist.

Beira was all too willing to have help, since she had more responsibilities now. She was no longer just the Old Woman of Winter, but an important fixture in Caoimhe's life.

She was accompanied by Old Man Snorfles when she chose to visit, bringing a biscuit tin filled with her own homemade sweets.

"After a certain age, women turn invisible," Beira said. "A solace to some. But for a goddess, the end of her existence. So we must be there for each other, throughout our lifetimes and the changes that will come."

"Maiden, mother, crone," said Leah. "One of those things that may be an invented tradition, but like other invented traditions, becomes tradition, all the same."

Caoimhe, Aoife, Beira, and Jenny Greenteeth.

"Women helping women," Jenny hissed.

So Caoimhe found herself with two new grandmothers willing to guide and teach her.

She was learning.

So were they all.

For Leah and Dorian, this case was closed.

***

Leah returned to her house in Faerie by the little warbling brook where the grasses moved in waves like the sea, green in the sunshine.

One day there was a knock at the door.

CHAPTER THIRTY-ONE

She opened it to discover Dorian Grey standing there.

"My apologies for not announcing myself, Miss Bishop," he said with a slight bow. "But I was unsure of the welcome I might receive."

"So you decided on the surprise attack?"

Leah held open the screen door.

"All's forgiven, Dorian. Come on in."

They sat together on Leah's porch as the sunset faded to gloaming, watching the time-between-times and the lavender night approach from the other side of reality.

"I never did talk to your landlord about squorbles."

"You can talk to Waffles tomorrow. We've got time."

Dorian raised his whisky glass.

Leah raised hers, too.

"We'll always have tomorrow, Dorian Grey."